IT'S NOT CONTAGIOUS.

Minutes passed.

Hours passed.

Of course she wasn't coming. She'd probably found a better friend already, somebody whose blood still circulated and whose skin didn't rot.

It was probably for the best, anyway. If Melody found out his secret—if *anybody* ever found out—his mother would throw a fit. And for good reason. A living dead boy would draw the attention of scientists with their sharp instruments and endless tests—assuming a mob of frightened neighbors didn't get to him first.

Nobody could ever know.

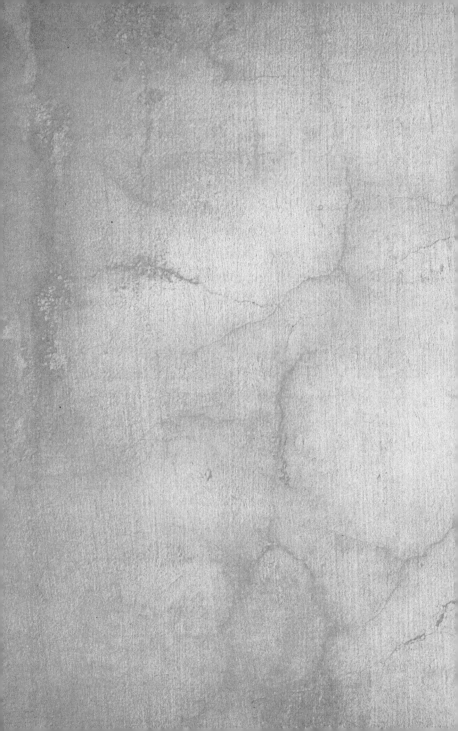

DEAD BOY

LAUREL GALE

A YEARLING BOOK

Text copyright © 2015 by Laurel Gale
Cover art and interior illustrations copyright © 2015 by Yoko Tanaka

All rights reserved. Published in the United States by Yearling, an imprint of Random House Children's Books, a division of Penguin Random House LLC, New York. Originally published in hardcover in the United States by Crown Books for Young Readers, New York, in 2015.

Yearling and the jumping horse design are registered trademarks of Penguin Random House LLC.

Visit us on the Web! randomhousekids.com

Educators and librarians, for a variety of teaching tools, visit us at RHTeachersLibrarians.com

The Library of Congress has cataloged the hardcover edition of this work as follows:
Gale, Laurel.
Dead boy / Laurel Gale ; illustrations by Yoko Tanaka. — First edition.
  pages cm.
Summary: Eleven-year-old Crow Darlingson has been dead for two years, forced to stay in the house with his overprotective mother except when he can sneak out, but new neighbor Melody Plympton offers a chance at friendship and, perhaps, getting his life back.
ISBN 978-0-553-51008-9 (trade) — ISBN 978-0-553-51009-6 (lib. bdg.) —
ISBN 978-0-553-51010-2 (ebook)
[1. Dead—Fiction. 2. Friendship—Fiction. 3. Magic—Fiction. 4. Supernatural—Fiction.
5. Shapeshifting—Fiction.] I. Tanaka, Yoko, illustrator. II. Title.
PZ7.1.G347De 2015 [Fic]—dc23 2014034081

ISBN 978-0-553-51011-9 (pbk.)

Printed in the United States of America
10 9 8 7 6 5 4 3 2 1
First Yearling Edition 2016

Random House Children's Books supports the First Amendment and celebrates the right to read.

To Mom and Dad

CHAPTER ONE

Being dead stank. Cuts didn't heal. Hair fell out and didn't grow back. Maggots burrowed in the stomach, which couldn't have digested anything anyway. And then there was the actual stink. The smell. The stench of rotting flesh. No matter how much spray-on deodorant Crow Darlingson used, he couldn't quite mask it.

Death was lonely, too. While other boys his age played ball in the street, he watched from his window. When they went off to school in the morning, he stayed home. But he still had to study and take tests; his mother saw to that.

"Can't we go outside?" he asked. "We can go into the backyard where nobody can see us."

Mrs. Darlingson, a slender woman with perfect

makeup and hair, shook her head firmly. "Too warm. Are you ready for your geography test?"

Anything much above forty degrees was too warm. Heat made the smell worse. Every once in a while, the Darlingsons' overworked air conditioner would break, and for days Crow's stink would spread throughout the block.

Maybe that was why the previous neighbors had moved, although they hadn't said anything. But leave they did, in quite a hurry, and now another family was taking their place. Crow could see the moving truck from his window. He could see the new family, too—a man, a girl, and a dog. The girl appeared to be around eleven, same as Crow, with short brown hair, plaid leggings, and a very bright tie-dyed T-shirt.

She looked up at the window, her head cocked to one side, and waved.

Crow waved back, shocked. Nobody had waved to him in years.

Mrs. Darlingson grabbed his hand, gently so it wouldn't fall off, and guided him away from the window. "Time for your geography test."

He aced his test, as always, even though it was a particularly hard one that involved drawing and labeling a map of Africa from memory. He made sure to spell each country, from Algeria to Zimbabwe, correctly.

School had never presented much of a challenge for

him. He'd helped his class win the academic bowl in the fourth grade, right before his death. He'd won the grade-level spelling bee that year, too, and would have gone on to compete against the fifth graders if he'd managed to stay alive for it.

Getting good grades was even easier without distractions like friends. Or food. Or fun. So of course he aced everything his mother placed in front of him.

Mrs. Darlingson put the test, marked with a bright red A+, on the refrigerator, where it joined the other quizzes and essays from that week. "Wonderful work. I'm so proud of you."

Crow shrugged. The motion caused the dry skin of his shoulders to crack, adding to the series of fissures already there. "What does it matter? It's not like I'll ever go to college."

"There are online colleges."

"It's not like I'll ever get a job."

"There are online jobs, too. You can do everything online these days." She smiled brightly.

Crow did not smile. "So I'm just supposed to stay inside this house forever? What's the point of studying geography if I'll never get to go anywhere?"

"You'll get to go out in a few weeks, just like you did last year. Don't you remember? You visited all the neighbors. You saw other children your age. You even got a bag full of candy."

"Halloween doesn't count." While the other boys

and girls dressed up as their favorite superheroes and vampires, Crow chose a costume to hide behind. And he couldn't actually enjoy any of the candy. His taste buds had rotted away years ago, and trying to eat just made the maggots worse.

He used to love Halloween. On the year before his death, he'd dressed up as an astronaut. His mother had sewn the space suit for him, and the costume was good enough to be used in the school play later that year. At least, it would have been used in the school play if he hadn't died first.

Now Halloween just reminded him of everything he'd lost. Maybe it was better to stay inside forever.

The doorbell rang.

Mrs. Darlingson frowned. "Stay here. I'll see who it is."

The doorbell never rang. Mrs. Darlingson, much like her son, had stopped having friends ages ago. Mr. Darlingson had friends, but even when he had still lived at home—before the divorce—they had never come to the house. A sign instructed solicitors to stay away, and another sign warned about a dangerous, but entirely fictional, dog. Packages weren't even sent to the house; they had a post office box for that.

Nobody came over, and that was just the way Mrs. Darlingson liked it. Only now somebody had come over. An impatient somebody, too—the bell rang a second time. A third time. Mrs. Darlingson's frown deepened as she walked to the door. Crow stayed in the kitchen, as ordered, although he did sneak a peek or two around the corner.

"I'm sorry. You must have the wrong house." She tried to shut the door, but something blocked it. Crow leaned forward to get a better view. A small foot was preventing the door from closing. He craned his neck and saw that the foot was attached to a girl. The girl who had waved at him. She had a friendly face, mostly freckles and smile, and long, lanky limbs that, judging by the way she fidgeted, she didn't seem to know what to do with.

"Of course I have the right house. I'm your new neighbor, Melody Plympton. I wanted to see who lived here—you know, make sure I hadn't moved next door to a bunch of ax-murdering psychos or spell-casting witches." She pushed the door open as far as Mrs. Darlingson would let her. "Why is it so cold?"

"I think the temperature's fine," Mrs. Darlingson said, although she was wearing a very thick wool suit and a pair of leather gloves. "I also think it's rude to ask questions like that. Or to assume that we're a bunch of ax murderers."

"Uh-huh. I saw a boy in the window. Where is he?"

"He's sick. In bed."

"No he's not." Melody pointed at Crow, whose head

was poking out of the kitchen. "He's right there. Why isn't he at school? I have today off because I just got into town, but he should be there."

"Well, if you knew where he was, why did you ask?" Before Melody could respond, Mrs. Darlingson added, "And he is sick, I'm afraid. Very sick. He can't have any company."

Melody rubbed her arms to warm herself. "Okay. I'll come back in a few days."

"No. He'll still be sick in a few days. And in a few weeks. Don't come back." Mrs. Darlingson forced the door shut, ignoring Melody's foot, still in the way, and Melody herself, who squealed in pain.

She locked the door, doorknob and dead bolt, before returning her attention to her son. "Ready for your geometry lesson?"

Silence fell over the house as midnight approached.

Crow made himself yawn. He did this once or twice every month, hoping the action of yawning would stimulate drowsiness, just as drowsiness stimulated yawning. It never worked. He hadn't slept in years. Not even one short nap. Not since he'd woken up from death. Before, back when his heart still beat, he'd spent his nights dreaming that he could fly through the universe or ride on a dinosaur. But no sleep meant no dreams. No more flying. No more dinosaurs. Just lots and lots of time.

So occasionally, and even though he knew his mother would be furious if she learned about it, he went downstairs in the middle of the night, opened the back door, and tiptoed outside.

Blaze, a small town in the middle of the Nevada desert, had temperatures in the eighties, nineties, and hundreds most of the year. During the day, Crow couldn't venture outside without his flesh giving off a putrid odor strong enough to make the maggots faint.

"Why don't we move somewhere cold?" Crow had suggested on numerous occasions. "North Dakota. Canada. The North Pole. Then I could go outside." Without having to sneak, but he had enough sense not to say that.

"We can't move," Mrs. Darlingson would say. "Our house is here." That was her favorite response, but she was also fond of bringing up how difficult the move would be. Before Mr. Darlingson had moved out, she'd given his job as an excuse. "It's not so bad, staying inside with me. Is it?"

And Crow knew that was the real reason she didn't want to move. She wanted him to stay inside with her. Always. Forever.

He couldn't do it. He needed out, if only for an hour a night.

Everyone was sound asleep by now, leaving no one to complain about the smell. Besides, on an early October night, it wasn't all that bad. In a few weeks, on

Halloween, Crow would even go out with his mother's permission. Other children would wrinkle their noses, but no one would faint. Hopefully.

Under Mrs. Darlingson's orders, Mr. Darlingson had taken down the old swing. The bike had been donated to charity. Pebbles had replaced the grass. Nothing remained to tempt Crow, except the fresh air and the stars. It was enough.

He stacked the pebbles in taller and taller towers. He searched for insects. Then he lay down and looked up at the stars.

Somewhere in the distance, an owl hooted.

Closer by, a fence creaked. Much closer. Someone was trying to open the Darlingsons' back gate.

A burglar, Crow thought. He wanted to run inside and tell his mother, but then he'd have to admit to sneaking out. His mother would seal the doors shut. She'd nail boards over his windows. He'd never see the stars again.

There was only one other option. He'd have to fight the burglar off himself. He grabbed a handful of pebbles, ready to pelt the intruder with them.

The fence wobbled. Someone was climbing up the other side. A head peeked over, and Crow threw his pebbles.

"Ouch!" Melody said, rubbing her shoulder where the pebble had struck her. She jumped down from the fence into the backyard. "What did you do that for?"

CHAPTER TWO

Crow stared at Melody. He had another pebble in his hand, aimed at her head. "I thought you were a burglar." He hesitated. "Are you?"

"Do I look like a burglar?"

Crow shook his head. She hadn't changed since that morning, and her plaid pants and tie-dyed T-shirt didn't exactly scream stealth. A burglar would have worn black, maybe with a ski mask and some gloves.

"I couldn't sleep," she explained. "New house and everything. Who knows what strange things are lurking in it. Rats. Ghosts. There has to be some sort of problem to explain how my dad bought it so cheap. Anyway, I looked out my window and saw you, and I thought you might need rescuing."

"Rescuing?"

She nodded. "Your mom was acting pretty strange, like she was hiding something. And if you're really as sick as your mom says, what are you doing in your yard in the middle of the night?"

"I couldn't sleep, either." He took a step backward, wondering how much of his sunken eyes and balding head she could see in the dim moonlight. "You said your name's Melody, right? I'm Crow Darlingson."

"That's a strange name." She took a step closer. "What do you have? Your mom said you'd be sick for a long time, so it can't be a cold or the flu. Is it mono? My older cousin got that from kissing a boy. She was sick for at least a month."

Crow took another step back. "No. It isn't mononucleosis." He'd done a report on the virus several months earlier, back when he'd been studying infectious diseases. Mononucleosis spread through close contact with other people, something he never had, so even if his dead body had been capable of catching it, he never would.

Frowning, she looked him up and down. "Is it a heart problem? My dad's best friend's sister has that."

Crow shook his head.

"Meningitis? Leukemia? TB? Polio? Tetanus? Leprosy? It's leprosy, isn't it?"

Crow shook his head for each of these.

"So what is it?"

"Generalized necrosis," he said. He quickly added, "It's not contagious."

"Oh, I'm not worried about that. I never get sick. Well, I had a cold a month ago. And I got the flu last year. And I get lots of ear infections. And pink eye. But other than that, I never get sick." With one more step forward, her toes were almost touching Crow's. She took a couple of sniffs. Her nose wrinkled.

"Sorry about the smell," Crow said. "It's the necrosis."

"That's okay. I have an uncle who smells way worse."

Crow smiled. The movement disturbed a maggot that had been sleeping in his left nostril. It woke up and wriggled out of his nose. His hands rushed to cover his face, but he feared it was too late.

"What was that?" Melody asked.

"Nothing," he said, his hands still hiding his face. "I should go inside. Try to sleep."

"Me too. But . . ." She paused. "I'll come back. Tomorrow night, same time, same place."

"Why would you do that?" The maggot was trying to wriggle its way into his mouth. He grabbed it and tossed it on the ground. Maybe, if he was lucky, Melody would think it was a booger.

Melody glanced at the spot where the maggot had landed, but it was dark, and she might not have been able to see anything. Her eyes returned to Crow, and she smiled. "I just moved here, and you have to stay home because of your neco . . . neca . . . ne . . ."

"Necrosis. Generalized."

"Right. Because of your generalized nec-whatever. So you're all alone, and I don't know anyone here yet, so I'm all alone, too. Maybe we could be friends." Her smile faded as she squinted at Crow. "Also, there's something strange about you. Something more than just being sick. I intend to find out what it is. I'll be back tomorrow. Don't throw any more pebbles at me."

"Oh. Okay."

The next night, Crow sneaked out of his house again. He was early, so he wasn't surprised to find that Melody hadn't arrived yet. He took advantage of the time by making sure his fingernails were glued on straight and his thinning clumps of hair covered as much of his head as possible. Best to look presentable for company.

Minutes passed.

Hours passed.

Of course she wasn't coming. She'd probably found a better friend already, somebody whose blood still circulated and whose skin didn't rot. She claimed not to mind the stink, but she must have been lying. An attempt at politeness, no doubt.

It was probably for the best, anyway. If Melody found out his secret—if *anybody* ever found out—his mother would throw a fit. And for good reason.

A living dead boy would draw the attention of scientists with their sharp instruments and endless tests—assuming a mob of frightened neighbors didn't get to him first. He'd read Mary Shelley's *Frankenstein* (an online copy, against his mother's wishes), so he knew how this sort of thing turned out.

Nobody could ever know.

The fence creaked.

Just the wind, Crow told himself. No reason to get excited. But he was excited. If his heart still beat, it would have been thumping in his chest. He turned to see what had caused the creaking.

Melody. She'd come after all.

"Sorry I'm late. I think one of my neighbors has been spying on me, so I had to wait until she went to bed."

"That's okay," Crow said.

They sat down on the ground. The backyard had no chairs or benches. Just lots and lots of pebbles. Crow wished he could offer something more comfortable, something that would make Melody want to stay, but short of dragging the sofa outside, there was nothing.

"I start school next week," Melody said. "I went there today, just to meet the principal and get my schedule."

"Oh. I . . . I bet you'll like it."

"I hope so. Have you ever been to Blaze Middle School?"

Crow shook his head. He'd attended Blaze Elementary, back when he was younger and still alive, but he'd never set foot in the town's middle school. He imagined it often, though. He pictured bright classrooms with smiling teachers. The students worked on group projects. They ate lunch together and played games after school. No one was ever alone. "You'll probably make lots of friends."

"Maybe." She got really quiet for a moment. Crow was about to ask what was wrong, but then she jumped up. "Let's play a game."

"Okay. What do you want to play?" Crow hoped it wouldn't be a word game. He played them all the time with his mother, and although he liked them well enough, they got boring after a while.

She hesitated. "Well, it's not exactly a game, but we could try to tell ghost stories. A dark night like this is the perfect time. I hear if you tell them while staring into a mirror, you might see a ghost."

"I don't know." Staring into a mirror was the last thing he wanted to do. Besides, the only scary story Crow could think of at the moment was his own, and sharing that didn't strike him as a good idea.

Melody nodded glumly. "Yeah, the kids in my old town thought it was lame, too."

"It's not lame. I just don't have a mirror."

"Okay, what about truth or dare?"

Crow shook his head. He had too many secrets for that.

"Do you have any video games or anything? Something you could bring out here?"

"No." He played games on his computer, but he couldn't bring that outside. He had a few board games, but most of them were word games, and anyway, he didn't want to risk going back inside. When it came to entertaining friends, he was totally unprepared. "Sorry."

Melody hesitated. "Well, it's a little silly with only two people, but sometimes I play charades with my cousins when they visit."

"That sounds fun. I'll go first. The category is books." He held up a finger to show that the title was one word. Then he lay down on the ground, got up, and started walking around with his arms extended in front of him.

"I have no idea, but, um, one word, so *The Borrowers*? *The Hobbit*? Wait, are you counting *the* as a word? Um, *Jumanji*?"

Crow motioned like he was screwing bolts into his neck.

"*Frankenstein!*"

"Yeah." Crow laughed. "I don't think the bolts were in the book, though. I don't remember them."

"You've actually read it? That's so cool. Okay, it's my

turn." She held up seven fingers. Then she crouched on the ground and opened her mouth in a silent roar.

"Seven words. A bear. A tiger. A lion."

Melody gave the last guess a thumbs-up. Next, she drew a triangle in the air and pretended to put the triangle on her head.

"A hat. A witch's hat. *The Lion, the Witch, and the Wardrobe!*"

They played a few more rounds before Melody said she had to go home.

"Will you come back tomorrow night?" Crow asked.

"As long as I can sneak out again."

The next night, Melody arrived shortly after midnight. Crow opened the gate for her, but she had already climbed halfway up the fence.

"My dad thinks I'm sick because I took a nap today, and I normally only do that when I have the flu. Maybe I can convince him that I can't start school for a while." She jumped down, nearly tumbling over but regaining her balance at the last second. "What about you? You're actually sick. Aren't you tired?"

Crow shook his head. "I don't sleep."

"Everyone sleeps. Even fairies and vampires."

But not whatever dead thing Crow was. He decided to change the subject. "Does your mom live with you? You haven't mentioned her, and I didn't see her when you were moving in."

Melody's face fell. "She had to, uh, she was—she's not here."

"Sorry. You don't have to talk about it if you don't want to."

"It's okay. I mean, it happened a long time ago. My mom disappeared when I was seven."

Crow sat down on the ground, and Melody sat next to him. "My dad doesn't live with me, either. He visits sometimes, but it's not the same. It stinks, doesn't it?"

"Yeah. Yeah, it stinks. I miss her a lot."

"I miss my dad, too," Crow said, wishing he'd picked a cheerier subject. "Hey, let's play charades again."

"You really like that game? The kids in my old town thought stuff like that was childish. They made fun of me a lot."

Crow shrugged. Before he'd died, he'd had lots of friends, and hardly anybody ever teased him. These days, though, he never played with kids his own age. He had no idea what was cool anymore. "It's fun. We can do something else if you want."

"I brought these." Melody pulled four small balls out of her pocket. They were rubber and glowed faintly green in the dark. "I'm learning how to juggle."

She juggled the balls, all four of them. After a while, she dropped one—on purpose, Crow thought—and juggled the other three in one hand.

Crow smiled. It reminded him of a show he'd seen

with his parents years ago, before everything—his own body included—fell apart. "That's cool."

"Want to try?" Without waiting for an answer, Melody threw him three of the balls, one at a time.

Crow barely managed to catch them, and they fell out of his stiff fingers as soon as he made an attempt to juggle.

"I couldn't do it at first, either." Melody took another ball out of her pocket. This one was squishy and didn't glow in the dark. "I'm learning magic, too. None of it is actual magic. They're just tricks. But I figure I'll come across something real if I keep looking, right?"

"I guess."

Through a series of quick movements, Melody made the squishy ball disappear and reappear in her hands. There wasn't much light, just what spilled over from the street lamps, but Crow saw enough to be impressed.

"What's that behind your ear?" She laughed. "Cheesy, I know, but it's a classic."

Before he could stop her, she reached behind his ear. When she retrieved the squishy ball, she took a clump of his hair with it. "Oh! I'm sorry!"

"It's okay." Crow glanced back at his house. Melody had made a lot of noise, and his mother might have heard. "It happens."

"Oh. Really? What did you say you were sick with?"

"Generalized necrosis." It was just a term he'd come up with, but it seemed pretty accurate.

Melody dropped the clump of hair on the ground and wiped her hands on her pants. "You should rest, I guess, even if you can't sleep."

"Yeah. Um, are you going to come back tomorrow?" He thought he might have scared her off.

"Of course. This is fun. I mean, not the hair part. Sorry about that. But you want me to come back, don't you? Am I bothering you? A lot of people say I bother them." She looked at the hair on the ground.

"Yes. I mean, no. No, you're not bothering me. Yes, I want you to come back." Other than the impossible wish of being alive again, he'd never wanted anything more.

Melody came back the next night, and the night after that. She showed him more magic tricks, and even taught him to juggle a little, and Crow found a deck of cards for them to play with. Mostly, though, they just talked.

"Your mom really makes you write ten-page reports?" Melody asked, right after he'd told her about the report he was doing on whether dinosaurs were endothermic or ectothermic, which he had to explain meant warm-blooded or cold-blooded. "And I thought regular school was bad."

"Regular school is much better. The reports aren't too bad, though, not when I get to pick the topics." His mother usually let him, as long as he challenged himself enough.

"Yeah, I'd write a report about Bigfoot or the Loch Ness Monster. There's a lot of evidence about them, but people keep trying to cover it up."

"You're really into magic and monsters and stuff, aren't you?" He wondered what she'd think if she learned the truth about him. Probably nothing good. Make-believe monsters were a lot easier to handle than real ones.

"Well, I told you that my mom disappeared." She hesitated. "Don't make fun of me, but I think it was because of magic. She always used to tell me stories about fairy queens and vampires and stuff, but I didn't believe any of it until one day—poof—she was gone. Just like that. I think she must have been involved in some sort of dangerous magical business, and the stories were supposed to be warnings. I mean, she wouldn't have just left, no matter what my dad says, so something strange had to have happened. And maybe if I learn enough about magic, I can figure out what happened, and I can bring her back. Hey—what's that in your ear?"

Before Crow could stop her, she reached out a hand

and touched the maggot squirming around his lobe. A short shriek escaped her lips. She jerked her hand away, hitting his ear in the process and knocking it loose from his head.

Crow grabbed his ear from the ground. "I . . . uh . . . I . . ."

"Wh-why aren't you bleeding?"

He didn't answer. His ear had just fallen off. No way would Melody want to be friends now. Nothing he could say or do would change that.

"I think I know what your secret is," she said. "You're dead."

Crow stayed silent. He'd had a friend for a few days. Really, that was more than he could have hoped for.

"You don't breathe. At first, I thought I was just imagining it—my dad says I imagine lots of things—but now I don't think so. You don't sleep, either. You said so yourself. Your hair falls out, your ear falls off, you smell, and I'm pretty sure that thing I just touched was a maggot. I looked up that disease you said you had. Generalized necrosis. The dictionary said *necrosis* means death. That's what's wrong with you, isn't it? You're dead."

Crow nodded, and another maggot crawled out of the hole where his ear had been. This time, he didn't bother trying to hide it. What would have been the point?

"But—how?"

"Does it matter?" Crow asked. He just wanted to go back inside and forget about this.

"Of course it matters. It's magic, isn't it?" She waited for Crow to say something, but he kept quiet. "I knew it! I knew magic was real! It has to be. Otherwise . . . otherwise . . . otherwise there are some things in this world that just couldn't be explained." She moved closer to get a better look at Crow, her head tilting from side to side as she attempted to view every angle of his dead form. "Does it hurt?"

He shrugged. At first, it had, but his nerves had rotted with the rest of him, and now he hardly felt anything. "Not really."

"Are you going to eat my brains?" She was looking at the maggot, now crawling down Crow's neck.

"No! I don't eat anything. Definitely not brains."

"Are you going to bite me? To make me one of you?"

"No. I told you. It's not contagious." He looked down at his hands, at the yellowed fingernails his mother had glued back on. "Listen, I understand if you don't want to be friends anymore. It's okay."

"Of course I want to be friends. I'm having more fun with you than I've had with anyone since . . . well, since my mom disappeared." Her smile faltered, but just for a second. "Besides, the only thing better than having a secret friend you have to sneak out to see is having a secret friend with a secret. It *is* a secret, isn't it?"

Crow nodded, too surprised to say anything. She really still wanted to be friends?

Melody stood. "I have to go, but I'll be back tomorrow night."

CHAPTER THREE

Mrs. Darlingson held her son's ear in her hand. "How did it fall off?"

"What?" Crow asked, even though he'd heard the question just fine; his ear continued to work even when it wasn't attached to the rest of his body. This was information best kept to himself, he decided.

"The ear!" Mrs. Darlingson yelled. "How did it fall off?"

He hesitated. "I don't know. It just did."

She nodded slowly, worry creasing her brow. Then, steeling herself, she took the ear and pressed it against her son's head. Up and down, left and right, she made small adjustments until it was in just the right spot. "You'll have to hold it while I sew."

Crow clutched the ear, careful not to move it. Lopsided ears just wouldn't do, not now that he had a friend. Which reminded him—he'd have to order a few more boxes of spray-on deodorant. Maybe he could get some new clothes, too. His were getting too small for him. He hadn't minded before, but now that Melody would be seeing him every night, a pair of pants that actually fit seemed in order.

He didn't understand why he kept growing every year. Frankenstein's monster hadn't done that. He would have asked his mother, but she didn't like to talk about these sorts of things.

Mrs. Darlingson picked up a needle, already threaded with surgical suture. She made small, tight stitches all around the ear. When she had finished, she tugged on the ear to make sure it didn't come loose.

"How does that feel?" she asked.

"Fine, I guess."

"Can you hear anything with it?"

He nodded. "I can hear fine. Good as new."

She tousled the few clumps of hair left on his head. "Do you want to start with Chinese history or American literature today?"

That afternoon, Mrs. Darlingson had to leave the house to run her weekly errands. Crow went up to his room to work on an essay about Chinese mythology. At least, that was what he told his mother. Really, he just wanted to be near his window so he could watch Melody coming home from her first day of school.

The bus pulled up to the sidewalk. Five children got off: Melody, two other girls, and two boys. Even from this distance, Crow could see that the girls were cute and the boys were tall. He could also see that, unlike himself, they were very much alive.

He recognized them, too. Most of them, anyway. Although it seemed like ages ago, it really hadn't been all that long since he'd been among them, a normal kid' getting off the bus after a normal day at school.

The two girls were Grace and Hannah. Crow had to think for a moment before he could remember who was who. When he'd been in school, it had always been Grace and Hannah, never just Grace, never just Hannah. The two of them might as well have been conjoined twins—cute, flawless ones.

Grace was the one with brown hair. She had been in a few local commercials for dental care, and she was always bragging about it. Hannah had blond hair, and she claimed some sort of connection to European royalty. Crow wasn't sure whether she was lying or not.

One of the boys was Luke. Crow had been in the school play and the spelling bee with him, though they had never been friends. Luke hadn't seemed to like Crow much, although Crow never could figure out why. Everyone else had liked Crow just fine. Whatever the reason, it made little difference now.

Crow didn't know the name of the other boy. He'd first appeared on the neighborhood sidewalks about a year ago, when his family must have moved into a house just a block or two away. When it wasn't too hot, he could be seen riding his bike, skateboarding, or annoying pigeons with Luke. Crow thought it looked fun—except for the bird-harassment part.

Melody waved good-bye to Grace, Hannah, Luke, and the other boy before skipping to her house.

She did not wave at Crow.

It didn't matter, Crow told himself. He couldn't expect her to wave at him every time she went outside. Except a wave wasn't all that difficult, was it? And she had waved to her new schoolmates. Her new friends.

Being Melody's best friend felt like a competition. Crow had gotten a head start, but he was already starting to lag behind. How was he supposed to compete with the living?

That night, the stars seemed especially bright. Crow quizzed himself on the constellations while waiting for Melody to arrive.

He didn't have to wait long. The fence creaked. Melody's head peeked over the wood panels. Every dead cell in Crow's body urged him to jump up, to run to greet her, but he forced himself to stay where he was, lying down on the ground. He didn't want to look too eager.

"Hey, Crow." She lay down next to him.

"Hey, Melody." He knew he should ask her about her first day of school. It was the obvious question. The polite question. But he couldn't bring himself to ask it. What if she'd had a wonderful time—so wonderful she didn't want to waste her nights with a dead boy anymore? What if all the fun had exhausted her and now she just wanted to go home and sleep?

"Are you ever allowed outside?" she asked. "Or do you always have to sneak out like this?"

"I always have to sneak. Except on Halloween. My mom lets me go trick-or-treating."

"That's great! We can go together!"

Crow smiled. "I'd like that."

"It's not right, though," she added. "You should be able to go outside. Meet other people. Just because you're dead doesn't mean you don't deserve a life."

Crow didn't say anything. He knew his mother was only trying to protect him, but he did get awfully bored. It wasn't like meeting people was much of an option, though. Melody might not care about the maggots, but most people would. Few people would put up with the stench.

Even his parents had to dab scented oil under their noses. They thought he didn't notice, but he did.

"What's it like?" Melody asked. "Being dead, I mean."

Crow shrugged. His heart didn't beat anymore, but it wasn't as if people normally paid that much attention to their pulse. Really, other than the decomposition, not much had changed. "A lot like being alive. Lonelier, though." And more maggoty, but he didn't want to gross her out by saying that.

"I know what you mean. I have a hard time making friends, too. When did you die?"

Crow had to think for a while. Days spent alone seemed like decades, but he knew it hadn't been that long. He'd died in the fourth grade. He was taking eighth-grade classes now, supplemented with whatever topics he or his mother found interesting, but that was only because he went through the material so quickly. If he still attended regular school, he'd be in the sixth grade. "A couple of years ago, I guess."

"How did you come back to life? Was it voodoo? Or a witch's spell? I've read all about witches."

"It wasn't a witch," Crow said. "I don't think it was. My parents just wished me back." He had heard his father call his mother a witch once, when they thought he couldn't hear, but he was quite sure the term had been used as an insult and not a description of any actual powers.

Sometimes he tried to remember his death. All he could recall was a horrible hiss—or was it a howl? Maybe it was good he couldn't sleep anymore. If he dreamed, he'd probably just have nightmares.

Melody nodded as if she knew all about wishes. "What did they tell everyone when you came back to life? Not the truth, right?"

"People knew that I'd died, so they couldn't hide that. They just said that I got better. They passed it off as a miracle, one of those cases where a patient is pronounced dead, but it turns out he was in a coma, and he recovers and everyone's happy. The doctors who examined me couldn't find anything wrong—I hadn't started rotting yet—although they did complain that it was hard to get a heartbeat. I went back to school for a couple of days, and I thought everything would return to normal. But then—"

He stopped. If his tear ducts had still worked, he might have cried.

"You started to rot," Melody said, finishing for him.

Crow nodded. "Yeah. Quickly, too. I tried to hide it at first, but it got too bad for that. My mom started homeschooling me. She told my friends I was too sick to play with them. They called and emailed a lot at first, then not so often, then not at all. My mom says it's a good thing, though. Having friends I can't hang out with would just make it harder."

"Well, you can hang out with me. What did you use to do with your friends?"

"Ride bicycles. Play video games. Collect bugs. Play baseball. Normal stuff." He'd never been lonely then.

"That sounds nice. Except for the baseball. I've

never been very good at sports. I don't like bugs, either."

Crow winced. "Sorry about the maggots."

"It's okay. I mean, as long as they don't get on me or anything, it's not a big deal."

They stared at the stars for a while. He identified the constellations for her while she told him about the aliens living on Mars.

"Wouldn't we know if there were aliens so close to us?" Crow asked. He'd read a lot about space, and he'd never come across any evidence of Martians.

"There's a big conspiracy to cover it up. I think the government wipes people's memories. I've probably had mine wiped loads of times. That's why I forget a lot of things, like when my homework's due, and that I'm supposed to make my bed in the morning."

"Oh," Crow said. "What do you think they look like?"

"I'm not sure. They're probably ugly, though. And scary. What do you think?"

"I bet they're green with tentacles." Crow liked the idea of something more monstrous than him.

The next night, Crow gave Melody a picture he'd drawn. It showed the two of them on Mars, talking to Martians.

"Thanks," Melody said. She frowned.

"What's wrong? Did I mess up the Martians?" Crow

had given them wings, which he thought looked really neat, but he wasn't sure that was right. Melody had said the Martians lived underground, and why would anything underground need wings? But they *did* look cool.

"It's perfect. But I don't have anything for you."

"Oh, that's all right. Just having you come here every night is more than I'd hoped for. It gets so lonely being stuck at home with no friends." He hesitated. Maybe it was better not to ask, not to make her realize that she was wasting her time with a putrid monster, but he had to know. As it was, he kept expecting her to yell *gotcha* and run away at any moment. "Why do you come here? I know you've made other friends."

"Yeah, they're okay, I guess. They're not magic." She looked at the drawing and smiled. "I've always known that magic, monsters, all of it, had to be real. Ever since my mom disappeared. You're proof."

"Oh," Crow said, fairly certain that she'd just called him a monster. And fairly certain she was right.

"Anyway, the other kids are boring. All they ever talk about is sports and makeup. You're way more fun, and you know, like, everything about everything."

"Not everything." Not according to his mother. For example, he'd only just started studying Chinese history, and he couldn't name more than two or three of the dynasties. He'd have to study more if he wanted to pass the tests she had planned.

Melody folded up the drawing and put it in her pocket. "Want to go somewhere?"

"Like where?"

She shrugged. "I don't know. But we're already sneaking out, so we might as well do it properly, right?"

"Okay. Where do you want to go? Las Vegas? The Grand Canyon?" He had some maps in his room, although he never thought he'd get to use them.

Melody paused. "Um, there's a park a couple of blocks away. Why don't we go there?"

"Oh. Yeah. Right. I was just joking about the Grand Canyon. Are you sure your dad won't get mad?" He knew his mom would, if she ever found out. Still, the opportunity was too tempting to pass up. The park! With slides and swings and everything.

"My dad's always mad at me for something," Melody said. "Might as well give him a reason. Besides, he'll only get mad if he finds out. We just won't get caught. Come on."

She started to climb over the fence, but Crow stopped her. He opened the gate, and they both walked through it.

Crow knew the sidewalks well. After all, he spent a good portion of his time staring at them from his window. But almost a year had passed since Halloween, when he'd last set foot beyond his yard.

Everything seemed different, like he was stepping

into a movie that he'd watched a million times. What had been flat and boring before now sprang into three-dimensional wonder.

"Are you okay?" Melody asked.

Crow realized he'd been standing still for several minutes now. "Yeah, fine. Let's go."

Shadows blanketed the empty streets. Other than their soft footsteps, nothing made a sound. No crickets chirped. No cars drove past. No wind blew through the trees, rustling the leaves. As Crow walked farther and farther from his house, he felt as if the world were watching him with bated breath.

The park was equally silent. Crow ran from sandbox to merry-go-round to slide, desperate to try everything at once. But his dead muscles weren't nearly as limber as live ones, and he didn't want to have to explain a fresh set of injuries to his mother. He settled on the swings, which seemed least likely to cause another body part to fall off.

Melody sat next to him, and they swung back and forth.

"How did you die?" she asked. "Were you murdered horribly? I bet you were murdered horribly. I want to hear all the details. Don't leave anything out, even if it's gruesome. Especially if it's gruesome."

"No. It was nothing like that. I was working on my dinosaur model one second, and the next second I was dead."

Melody stopped swinging. "But what killed you?"

"I don't know."

"How did you come back to life? Your parents wished you back, but how?"

"I don't know." He didn't want to waste the night talking about his death. "What's Blaze Middle School like?"

She shrugged. "Okay, I guess. I think my history teacher is a warlock. And I'm pretty sure they're putting some sort of poison in the cafeteria food. I'll have to bring lunches from home from now on."

"Huh? Why would a warlock get a job teaching? And why would he poison the food?"

"Well, he talks about the Renaissance like he was actually there, and he's super old, too, and his class passes really slowly. I mean *really* slowly. I bet he has magic that lets him control time. But I don't think *he's* poisoning the food. Somebody is, because it tastes really funny, but it's not necessarily him."

Crow still didn't think that seemed very likely. She seemed so confident, though, that he didn't want to start a fight by saying anything. He had to be careful until he got the hang of this friend business.

Which reminded him.

"What about your new friends?" He hoped he'd managed to keep the jealousy out of his voice. "I saw you the other day. You were waving to Grace, Hannah, Luke, and the other kid. I don't know his name, but I've seen him before, ever since he moved here last year. Not that I watch him. I wasn't watching you, either. I was just looking out my window, and there aren't a lot of places to look, so I saw you, and—"

"It's okay. The other boy is Travis. He and Luke are nice, I guess. Well, not *nice*. Funny, though. A little loud. Luke got detention today because he kept making fun of the teacher every time he turned around. I think the teacher has eyes in the back of his head—literally—because he saw Luke and sent him to the principal's office. And why would anyone have a combover like that unless they had something to hide?"

"What about the girls, Grace and Hannah?"

Melody shrugged. "They want to give me a makeover. They say we can pretend like I'm on one of those reality TV shows. I don't know if I should do it. They want to dye my hair and pierce my ears, and I don't think my dad would go for that. He won't even let me wear lip gloss, although they say I can put it on when I get to school. What do you think? Should I let them make me over?"

"No. I mean, if you want to, you should, but I don't think you need to. I think you look fine." He liked her freckles and her big toothy smile.

"Thanks." She winced. "Sorry. I have to go home now."

"Can't we stay just a little longer?" He didn't have a watch, but he was sure it wasn't that late. Something else had to be wrong. "Is it because I smell? I ran out of deodorant, so I used my mom's perfume, but I guess I used too much, and she made me wash it off—"

"No. It's not that. I put a little rose oil under my nose. I can't smell anything else."

Crow nodded. His parents did that, too. "Then why do you want to go?"

"I have to use the bathroom."

"Oh." He looked over at the small building at the edge of the park. "Isn't there a bathroom here?"

"I guess, but it's probably locked. It's getting late, anyway, and tomorrow's a school day."

Crow jumped off his swing and ran toward the small building. If it wasn't locked, he might convince her to stay awhile longer. He pulled at the handle, but the door didn't budge. A chain kept it firmly in place.

But there was still a way in.

A rectangular panel was missing from the bottom third of the door. Once it had probably been a vent, but now it was just a big hole. Big enough to crawl through. And that was exactly what Crow did.

"Wait!" Melody said. "That's not the bathroom! I think it's a storage shed."

The information came too late. Crow was already inside. His hand fumbled for the light. He found the switch, covered in spiderweb, and flipped it on. Nothing happened. On, off, on, off, but the darkness held steady.

Melody crawled through the hole.

Crow could see just enough to realize there wasn't much to see. The room was almost empty. Almost.

Something hissed.

"What was that?" Melody asked.

Something growled.

"I don't know," Crow said. But it sounded familiar.

Another hiss. A howl. A squawk. Judging by the chorus of animal sounds, an entire zoo was hiding in the tiny building.

"Let's get out of here," Melody said. She tugged at his shirt.

"Wait." He stepped farther into the shed. He'd been here before. He was sure of it. He just didn't know when or why.

Melody scrambled outside.

Crow stayed. His eyes strained against the darkness. Snarls, bleats, croaks, and roars struck his ears, but he could see only a single figure scurrying in the shadows. In the darkness, he couldn't tell what it was.

A memory came to him. His eyes were opening for the first time after the deepest, darkest sleep. His parents stood over him, their faces streaked with tears. And there was someone else, too. No, *something* else. A creature. A monster.

The same monster that chattered and cawed in the storage shed.

CHAPTER FOUR

The monster continued its screeching, growling, and hissing. The noise filled Crow with dread. He remembered very little about what had happened two years ago, but it was enough to convince him that this creature, whatever it was, had played a role in his current dead state. And what sort of monster could make a boy rot and crumble the way Crow did?

An evil one.

Besides, the animal sounds were frightening enough on their own. It seemed like there were at least a hundred beasts in the tiny shed, and every single one of them sounded hungry.

In his rush to escape, Crow scraped his knee against the edge of the hole in the door. His skin tore. A chunk of his flesh, almost completely detached, flapped against the rest of his leg, but this didn't slow him down. He scrambled the rest of the way through, almost somersaulting as he stumbled outside.

Inside the building, the creature mewed and hissed and bellowed. Crow didn't wait to see if the thing inside would emerge. He bolted.

Death and disuse had weakened his muscles. He hadn't run in years, and now that he needed to, his legs wouldn't go fast enough. Melody sped ahead. He'd be left alone in the park, he realized, and the creature would devour him.

But after a backward glance, Melody slowed down. Crow caught up to her.

"What was that?" she asked, out of breath and wide eyed.

"I—I don't know." Not exactly. But he was sure it was something horrible. "Let's go home."

She nodded. They walked down the dark sidewalks, glancing over their shoulders again and again. Nothing followed them—at least, nothing they could see. But Crow still felt a pair of eyes watching him. He still heard the strange growling and hissing. Maybe it was simply the memory of the sounds echoing in his mind. Maybe not. He quickened his pace as much as his dead legs would allow.

Soon they reached their block. The porch light at Crow's house was on. Mrs. Darlingson stood outside. There was a man, too, whom Crow did not recognize.

For a moment, a sense of relief overwhelmed Crow. Adults were there. They would keep him and Melody safe. Then Mrs. Darlingson started yelling, and the comfort vanished.

"Where have you been? I've been worried sick! You know you're not allowed out of the house." She paused, looking at the stranger, and added, "At night. Something horrible could have happened."

Crow stared at the ground, unable to look his mother in the eyes. "I'm sorry. I just wanted to go to the park."

"But at midnight!" the man said. "We were about to call the police. What were you thinking, Melody? This isn't like you."

"Sorry, Dad." She paused. "How did you know I was with Crow?"

The man—Mr. Plympton, Crow realized—clenched his jaw. His nostrils flared. "A neighbor called. She saw you coming over here. But that's not really the point, is it? What were you thinking?"

Melody lowered her head. "Sorry."

"Your leg!" Mr. Plympton said.

Crow looked up. Mr. Plympton was pointing at Crow's leg with a trembling finger.

"We'd better call an ambulance." He fumbled in his pocket and fished out a cell phone.

"No!" Mrs. Darlingson yelled, startling Mr. Plympton and causing him to drop his phone. "No ambulances, please. We have our own doctor. Crow has a special skin condition."

"What's that coming out of his wound? Are those worms?" Mr. Plympton's cheeks puffed up slightly, like he was about to vomit.

"No. Don't be silly." Mrs. Darlingson brushed the maggots away from Crow's leg, careful not to tear the skin off any further. "Just some dirt. We'd better get inside and take care of this. Thank you for alerting me to the trouble tonight."

"But . . . are you sure . . . an ambulance . . ." He looked Crow up and down. Even in the dim glow of the porch light, he no doubt noticed Crow's thin hair and sunken eyes. He was close enough to notice the smell, too, even if it was a cool night.

"What disease does your son have?" He grabbed Melody's hand and took a step back, yanking her away from Crow. "Is it contagious?"

"Yes," Mrs. Darlingson said.

Crow's mouth fell open.

Melody twisted her hand free of her father's. "No, it's not! She's just saying that because she doesn't want Crow to have friends."

"I don't want you to be friends with Crow, either," Mr. Plympton said, taking hold of his daughter's hand again. "Not if this is the sort of behavior I can expect from the two of you. You've really disappointed me, Melody."

He grabbed Melody by the arm and dragged her back to their house.

Crow sat in the kitchen, his injured leg propped up on a chair, while Mrs. Darlingson stitched up the wound. For a long time, Crow stayed silent, anger flowing inside him the way blood used to.

"You lied," he said at last.

Mrs. Darlingson kept her eyes on her work. "Do you mean about your being contagious? It was for your own good. Someday, when you're older, you'll understand."

"But it was a lie! You shouldn't lie like that. It's not right."

After pausing to remove some maggots that had squirmed to the surface, she completed a few more stitches and put the needle down. "You run away in the middle of the night, leaving me to worry, and now *you're* mad at *me*? No. That's not how it works."

"I wasn't running away. I was just going to the park. I can't stay inside forever."

"You can, Crow. And more than that, you should. It's what's best for you." She picked up the needle and resumed stitching. "You need a punishment, of course. I think an essay is in order. Five pages detailing why it's dangerous for an eleven-year-old boy to wander the streets at night. You can do it tomorrow, along with your regular schoolwork. Maybe by the time you finish, you'll understand how worried I was."

Crow hung his head. He'd only wanted to see something beyond the walls of his house. He hadn't meant to make his mother upset.

"I even called your father."

"You did?" Crow sat up straighter. "Is he coming over?"

"No. I texted him not to when I saw you walking back. Good thing, too. You know it's a two-hour drive, and he has to work tomorrow." She finished the last stitch and cut the thread.

"Oh." Of course his father wasn't coming over. Mr. Darlingson only visited once or twice a month, less often if things got busy at the office. Which they often did.

Crow looked at his mother, whose eyes were red and puffy, whose cheeks were streaked with tears. Then he looked at himself: his icy hands with yellowed nails glued on, his stitched-up knee, the maggot crawling around his ankle. No wonder his father had decided to leave. Who would want to live with a rotting corpse? "I'll try to be better. I'll use more deodorant. And I won't sneak out again. I promise. Then will Dad visit more?"

"Crow, sweetie, our separation has nothing to do with you." She gave his shoulder a gentle squeeze. "Your father loves you, and so do I. We just weren't happy as a couple. Now, it's late, and I'm tired. We can discuss this more in the morning. I trust you won't try to go back outside tonight?"

"No," Crow said. He kissed his mother good night, dragged himself up to his bedroom, and wished the events of the last hour could be undone.

CHAPTER FIVE

Crow knew that his mother had been right: it was dangerous for an eleven-year-old boy to wander the streets at night. And he knew why: there were monsters out there. With everything that had happened, he'd almost forgotten about the horrible growls and squawks. Now, sitting alone in his room, the dark night pressing against his window, he could think of nothing else.

He'd seen the monster before. It had hovered over him when he'd first awoken from death. Why? He tried to remember more about it. What did it look like? What had it done? But his foggy memory was no help. All he knew was that the monster was somehow involved in—somehow responsible for—his lonely existence as a walking corpse. It was powerful and terrible and it lived just a couple of short blocks away.

So it was dangerous to leave the house at night.

But he couldn't put that in the paper his mother was making him write, not without upsetting her even more. She didn't like it when he mentioned his death—as if not talking about the past could improve the present.

Instead, he looked up information on accidents and crimes. The Internet provided him with more than enough horror stories involving kids who ran away from home and wound up abducted, hit by a car, or simply lost forever. By the time the horizon turned pink with the rising sun, he had the five pages he needed.

A bird sang outside. Or maybe it wasn't a bird. The monster had used the voices of dozens of animals. If it could sound like a lion or a snake, it could probably sound like a sparrow or a warbler, too.

The sun didn't make Crow feel much safer. Monsters had to get hungry during the day, too. And the light didn't make the park storage shed any farther away.

Despite this fear, a desire grew in Crow's unbeating heart. He wanted to return to the park. He didn't remember much about the monster, but he was sure it had been there when he'd returned from the dead. Scary or not, the monster might have answers, and Crow had so many questions.

Crow couldn't eat, and Mr. Darlingson was gone, but Mrs. Darlingson insisted on dinner as usual. Chicken breasts simmered in mushroom sauce. Asparagus steamed until tender. Red potatoes roasted with garlic. It seemed like a lot of work for one person's meal, but that was the price of normalcy.

The food smelled delicious. Crow couldn't eat, couldn't taste, couldn't digest, but he could smell. The wonderful scents tormented him. He wanted to try a bite—just a small one. Surely one little potato wouldn't hurt. But experience had taught him better. One little potato really would hurt. The food would sit in his stomach until it rotted. The maggots would multiply out of control. The stench would worsen. Worst of all, without any remaining taste buds, he wouldn't even be able to enjoy the food.

The phone rang. Mrs. Darlingson answered it. A moment later, without saying a word, she hung up.

"Who was that?" Crow asked, wondering whether she would hang up on his father. He didn't think she would, but he hadn't thought they'd separate, either.

"A telemarketer. I wish they'd stop calling." She set two places at the table, then removed one, sighing and shaking her head.

Crow took his seat and did his best to smile.

"Did you read anything interesting today?" she asked.

"Mark Twain's real name was Samuel Clemens." He hesitated. She wasn't going to like this, but he had to try. "How did you and Dad bring me back from the dead?"

"So he used a pen name. How inter—" She put her fork down. "Why are you asking about that? We've already told you everything you need to know. Your father and I wished for you to return to us."

"But I make wishes all the time, and they never come true." Otherwise he would have had a pet dinosaur since he was seven and a helicopter since he was eight. He'd have an endless supply of candy that he could actually eat and friends he could hang out with whenever he wanted, no sneaking required. Most of all, he'd have his life back. He didn't have any of these things, proof that wishing didn't work.

"It was a very special wish," Mrs. Darlingson explained. "One powered by our love."

"Did someone help you? Or something?"

Mrs. Darlingson's brow wrinkled as she looked at her son. "Last night, when you were with that dreadful neighbor girl, where did you say you went?"

"The park. We played on the swings."

She nodded slowly. "And while you were there, did you see . . . anything?"

"No. I didn't see much of anything," Crow said, selecting his words with great care. He didn't like to lie to his mother, not if he could help it. She always seemed to know. "Don't try to change the topic. Did you and Dad get help with your wish?"

"I'll change the subject if I want. This is my house. Now, if you help me with the dishes, I'll let you watch television this evening."

"You mean a documentary?" That was all he ever got to watch.

"No. Anything you want."

"Okay," Crow said. He still wanted to know about the monster, but talking to his mother wasn't going to get him anywhere. Luckily, she wasn't the only one he could ask.

Before Crow's death, he'd always been close to his father. Immediately after he was brought back, little changed. On the Friday evening after the wish, the Darlingson family went bowling, just as they had every Friday evening before. At the time, Crow seemed perfectly normal and healthy, with only a couple of minor exceptions, little things like the heartbeat that no one could find and the sleep that wouldn't come. The maggots and the stench hadn't developed yet.

"We could try another sport," Mrs. Darlingson said, wrinkling her nose at the rental shoes. "Golf, for instance. Miniature golf, if you insist. Anything without smelly footwear."

"For the last time, Caroline, we like bowling." Mr. Darlingson turned to Crow. "Do you remember the techniques I taught you?"

Crow nodded. He'd been practicing at home, even

though he didn't have a bowling ball and could only pretend to bowl. "Can we get some soda and nachos before we start?" He didn't actually feel hungry or thirsty, but he loved nachos and root beer.

"No," Mrs. Darlingson said. "The food here is disgusting, and soda will rot your teeth."

In hindsight, it was a pretty ridiculous concern.

Mr. Darlingson and Crow started playing, while Mrs. Darlingson disinfected her shoes and bowling ball. When it was Crow's turn, Mr. Darlingson disappeared, but he returned in time to see his son's spare.

"Nice job." He handed Crow a soda and added in a whisper, "Don't tell your mom. She's still mad at me because I used her eyeliner as a pencil. And because I fell asleep when she was telling me about—about—I don't remember. Something. Anyway, I don't need to give her another reason to yell at me."

Crow laughed.

They bowled a few more rounds, Mrs. Darlingson scowling every time she saw Crow take a sip of soda. It was fun until Crow's stomach turned sour. He threw up, and the night was ruined.

Not just the night.

Crow waited until his mother had gone to sleep. He didn't expect Melody to meet him in the backyard, not so soon after they'd gotten caught, but he'd check anyway. First, though, he was going to the kitchen.

He picked up the phone and dialed his father's number.

It rang and rang. Finally, Mr. Darlingson answered. "Caroline, what's wrong? Did Crow leave the house again?"

"No, it's me. I—I just wanted to talk."

"Oh, hey, kiddo. I want to talk to you, too, but it's really late. Can I call you tomorrow? Or I'll be coming to visit you in a little while, and we can talk then."

"No. It needs to be when Mom isn't around. I want to know about the wish the two of you made. The one that brought me back. Did you get help?" When his father didn't answer immediately, Crow added, "You know how Mom can be sometimes. She never wants to talk about anything, and she doesn't get how important this is to me, but you do, don't you? You know I'm old enough to know what happened when I died."

Crow considered calling him the coolest dad in the world, but decided that would be taking the flattery a little too far. Playing his parents off each other was a fine art.

Mr. Darlingson paused so long that Crow was starting to think the line had gone dead. But finally, he said, "I guess you do have a right to know. I always thought we should be more open with you. Yes. There was a creature. A Meera, it was called. A shape-shifter. It granted our wish."

So Crow's suspicions had been right. The monster

in the storage shed had seemed familiar for good reason. It was the Meera, the creature that had brought
Crow back to life—if such a state as his could be called
living.

"Was it evil?" Crow asked. The way it grunted and
croaked, it had to be. He shuddered at the memory of
all those sounds.

"No. No, of course not. Nothing about your returning to us was evil, Crow."

A million questions raced through Crow's head.
"What is the Meera? Why did it grant your wish?
Why did it make me like this, still dead and rotting?"

Once again, Mr. Darlingson did not answer immediately. "The Meera is a sort of judge. Some people go
to it willingly, like your mother and me. Others are
forced. There are tests. Those who fail are punished—
assuming they survive. Those who pass receive a wish.
We asked for you to come back to us, to be given the
chance to grow up." He hesitated. "I guess we probably should have worded the wish a little more carefully. We just assumed that you'd come back alive."

Crow let the information sink in. For years, he had
wondered why he grew taller every year, even though
his dead body shouldn't have been capable of growth.
Now he knew. It was what they had wished for.

"Why didn't you make another wish?" Crow asked.

"We tried that. The Meera said that a person could
only earn one wish. Since your mother and I both

asked for you to return, both of us had used up our wish. We couldn't get another."

"Could I?"

"No. Definitely not. Your mother might be a little overprotective sometimes, but she only wants to keep you safe. Promise me you won't sneak out again. Promise me you won't try to find the Meera."

"Why not? You said it was good."

"No, I said it wasn't evil. Please, promise me you won't try to find it."

"I promise," Crow said. Luckily, his father couldn't detect lies the way his mother could.

CHAPTER SIX

Melody spent more and more time with her new friends Grace and Hannah. They rode their bicycles together, while Crow watched from the window. She waved once in a while, but not very often.

Be happy for her, Crow told himself. She deserved friends. But so did he, and now that his only friend had deserted him in favor of the living, he just couldn't make himself feel happy for her. Wishes kept popping into his head—horrible wishes involving the two new friends. Their hair would fall out in clumps. Maggots would infest their ears. Their flesh would rot off, leaving nothing but a skeleton. Most importantly, Melody would run away screaming.

He didn't actually want these things to happen. Not really. Not most of the time. But he couldn't stop imagining them, either. Would the monster in the storage shed, the Meera, grant wishes like these?

He'd been working up the courage to go back to the park. Not to ask the Meera to torture Grace and Hannah. Just to talk to it. To see what it knew about his death. He had to talk to someone, even if that someone was a monster, and talking to his mother was getting him nowhere.

"How did I die?" he'd ask.

And she'd respond with something like, "Can you hand me that pen?" It didn't matter that another pen lay on the desk mere inches from her fingers.

Later, he'd try again, and she'd say something like, "Oh, look at the time. I'd better get dinner started." It could be four o'clock, and she'd still talk about getting dinner ready.

Even worse, sometimes she wouldn't respond at all, as if Crow were a ghost no one could hear. Being dead was bad enough without being ignored.

He'd tried calling his father again, but his father had said that some things needed to be discussed in person, so the conversation would have to wait until his next visit. Except that wouldn't be for days, and Crow needed answers now. And even when his father finally did visit, his mother would hover over them, as she always did. They wouldn't have any time alone. If Crow asked about his death, she would probably announce that it was time for bed. His father would leave, and Crow would have learned nothing.

He missed his father. He missed their basketball matches at the park and their Friday-night bowling competitions. He missed the camping trips they'd gone on. But all of that had been years ago, before Crow's death. Even if Mr. Darlingson hadn't moved out, things like sports and camping wouldn't be possible, not for a dead boy who couldn't leave the house.

His life had been stolen from him, and no one would even tell him why.

The Meera would have the answers his parents refused to give him.

Mrs. Darlingson had put bells on the front and back doors, ones that would clang loudly if he tried to leave. She'd forgotten about the windows, though. The one in the living room made a convenient exit once the screen was removed. Crow knew because he'd done it every night in the last week, every night since he and Melody got caught coming home from the park.

Careful not to make a sound, Crow tiptoed downstairs. He opened the window, put the screen aside, and slipped outside.

That night, like every night, he waited for Melody until two o'clock—not out of hope, but out of habit. He didn't really expect her to come. When proven right for the seventh night in a row, his disappointment was mild. He pushed it to the back of his mind. Really, it was better that she hadn't come tonight. Crow wouldn't have wanted to bring her along on his dangerous mission. He opened the gate as quietly as he could, moving slowly so it wouldn't creak.

The partially cloud-covered moon offered little light. Crow tried to assure himself that this was, in fact, a good thing. It meant nobody could see him. But it also meant he'd have to confront the Meera in almost-perfect darkness, something he'd rather not do.

Mr. Darlingson had said the Meera was neither good nor evil, just like the wild animals whose voices it mimicked. And wild animals, being neither good nor evil, had a habit of eating people when given the chance. Would the Meera do the same?

Maybe not. Crow wasn't very appetizing, after all. A vulture or hyena might consider him a decent snack, but other animals would likely leave him alone.

Crow's eyes widened. He thought he remembered a strange cackling laughter mixed in with the howls and meows from his first night at the park. It could have been the sound of a hyena. Or maybe his memory was playing tricks on him. There was no way to be sure.

He'd reached the park.

His feet refused to move any farther. Turn back, he told himself. Go back home, where it's safe and secure.

Safe and secure and lonely. He couldn't go back

home, not without finding the answers he needed. He wanted something else, too—something more important than information.

If the Meera had granted his parents' wish, maybe it would grant his, too.

There was only one way to find out. He forced his feet forward.

Something chattered in the darkness. He kept moving toward the storage shed.

Buzzing. Braying. Gibbering. How could the neighbors not hear the cacophony of animal sounds? Or maybe they did hear, but they chose to ignore the frightening noises. If that was the case, would they also ignore a child's screams?

The maggots in his stomach twisted into knots, but Crow kept walking forward. He reached the storage shed. All he had to do was climb through the hole where the vent used to be.

It was like saying all he had to do was move a mountain. It wasn't that easy.

He bent down. Something croaked. He put one leg through the hole. Something cawed. He put his head and shoulders through. Something hooted. He stood up in the shed, and a deafening howl almost knocked him over. Stumbling against the locked door, he shoved his fingers in his ears.

"I-i-it's me, C-c-crow Darlingson. You m-met my parents." The howl died down, and Crow stood up straighter. "C-could you tell me about what happened?"

For a moment, the room was dark and quiet. Then a roar ripped through the silence. A small spark burned briefly before exploding into a stream of flame. The bright fire illuminated a horrible shape crouching in the small shed: a large snout, red eyes, sharp teeth, wings, and a tail. A dragon! It barely fit inside the small room, its body bent and twisted into every available space.

The tail shot toward Crow like a whip. Another blast of fire singed his few remaining clumps of hair. The air vibrated with the dragon's roar.

Crow ran out of the hole in the door. He didn't stop running until he was back in his living room.

CHAPTER SEVEN

To explain away his scorched hair, Crow made up a story about attempting a science experiment in the middle of the night. He'd done such things in the past, during his many sleepless hours, so it wasn't that strange for him to decide to calculate the calories in a walnut at midnight.

Anyway, his story was more believable than the truth. A dragon lived in the storage shed at the park.

Even Crow didn't believe it, and he'd seen the thing with his own terrified eyes. Still, he knew it hadn't been a real dragon. Sure, it looked like a dragon. It breathed fire like a dragon. But it had been the Meera, he was certain, and the dragon was just one of its many forms.

A shape-shifter, his father had said.

That didn't make it any less frightening. No, no, not at all.

With so many thoughts screaming in his head, Crow decided it was best to stay busy. He finished his schoolwork—a geometry quiz, a geography quiz, a science experiment to measure the freezing point of water with various levels of salt, and a paper on *The Adventures of Huckleberry Finn*—before noon. Then, unable to sit still, he began cleaning.

Unfortunately, Mrs. Darlingson kept a tidy house, always vacuuming and dusting to keep the maggot infestation at bay, so Crow had to look pretty hard before finding any sort of mess. He stood on a chair and dusted the top of the refrigerator. His hand slid into the small gap between the cabinet and refrigerator, where it found a dead cockroach.

Oh! Not dead! The bug skittered out of his reach.

Or maybe it wasn't a bug. Crow shuddered. Maybe it was the Meera in a new form. If it could turn itself into a huge dragon, it could turn itself into a tiny cockroach, too.

But it was probably just a bug. And Crow just needed to keep busy.

He tackled the phone next. According to an article he'd read, telephones harbored millions of germs. Being dead, he was immune to viruses, but his mother wasn't. He disinfected the phone, the answering machine, and even the wire that plugged into the phone jack.

Except it didn't plug into the phone jack.

Crow stared at the wire. This wasn't right at all.

"Mom!" he yelled. "What happened to the phone?"

"What? Nothing! What are you talking about?" She hurried into the kitchen, where her son showed her the severed wire. "Oh, that. I, uh, accidentally cut it while I was chopping vegetables for dinner. I'll get a new one soon enough."

"But what if Dad calls?"

"If it's important, he'll stop by the house. Or he'll email us. Or he'll call me on my cell phone. Really, I don't know why I've kept the landline. It's so unnecessary these days, don't you think?"

Crow nodded slowly, his forehead creased. How had she managed to cut the wire while chopping vegetables? The phone was nowhere near the counter space she used to prepare food.

Mrs. Darlingson smiled. "You've done enough cleaning and studying for one day. Why don't you go up to your room for a while and do something fun? You haven't worked on your knots for a long time. Why don't you practice your figure eights or butterfly knots? Or you could finish your airplane model. That thing's been collecting dust for months now."

Crow nodded again and went upstairs. He didn't

feel like tying knots, though. He didn't want to work on his model airplane, either, or his chemistry set, or his loom, or any of the scores of other educational diversions his mother had bought for him over the years. But he was supposed to start *Gulliver's Travels* that week, so he sat next to the window and opened his book. The words on the page blurred, his mind unwilling to focus.

Outside, the school bus pulled over to let its passengers off. Melody emerged, followed by Grace and Hannah, her two new friends. Best friends, probably. The two boys, Luke and Travis, got off next. While the bus drove away, all five of them stayed behind to talk and laugh. No one was in a hurry to go home, not with the sun shining so bright.

No one bothered to look up at Crow's window. No one waved.

Melody had forgotten him.

He threw down his book. The living room had been gathering some clutter. He went downstairs and began sorting through the copies of *Popular Science, National Geographic,* and *Time.* The newer ones stayed out, while the older ones were moved into the closet and alphabetized. Little space remained, but he refused to throw anything out. He might need it someday. Besides, what other contact with the outside world could he manage? Sure, he had the Internet, but he wanted something he could touch, something another person had held at some point. It felt more real that way.

He'd have to make more room. A large cardboard box was taking up a lot of space. He peered inside and found it empty except for some unopened letters lining the bottom. Odd. Why would his mother keep the letters but not bother to open them? He picked one up to see who had sent it.

The door opened.

"What are you doing out here?" Mrs. Darlingson demanded. "You're supposed to be playing in your room."

"I got bored." He stared at the letter in his hands. "Why didn't you give this to me?"

Mrs. Darlingson marched over. She attempted to snatch the letter from Crow's grip, but he held on tight. She reached toward the box, but he was closer. He grabbed the other letters before she could get to them.

Suddenly everything made sense. Crow stared at his mother as if seeing her for the first time.

"You cut the phone line on purpose, didn't you?" he asked. "Because Melody kept calling. It wasn't a telemarketer. It was her."

"Give me the letters." She held out her hand.

Crow clutched the letters to his chest. "No. They're mine. Melody sent them to me."

"I'm your mother. I know what's best for you."

"You don't!" Crow yelled, the anger in his voice surprising him. "You think you know what's best, but you don't. Dad would understand. He'd let me see the letters."

"Your father isn't here. I am." Mrs. Darlingson's voice remained calm. "But even if he were, he'd agree with me. The world isn't ready for you, Crow."

"Then you shouldn't have brought me back."

Still holding the letters, he stomped past his mother to the door. She grabbed hold of his right arm, trying to stop him. He pushed her away. She didn't let go. He kept walking, holding the letters in his left hand, while his right arm tore off at the shoulder.

It didn't matter. They could sew it on later. Right now, he had some letters to read.

CHAPTER EIGHT

Crow's body parts were falling off at an alarming rate. Rather than wait for another arm or leg to detach, Mrs. Darlingson decided to reinforce all of his joints with sutures. "I learned a new stitch," she explained. "It's meant to make clothes durable, but it should work on you, too."

The entire process took several hours, and Crow didn't say a word to her the entire time. He was still thinking about the letters. None of them had stamps on them. Melody must have placed them in the Darlingsons' mailbox herself.

She had written every single day following their midnight trip to the park. She hadn't forgotten him after all. When he wasn't being mended like an old doll, he read each letter over and over, savoring the smallest details. She'd gone back to the park a couple of times but never heard the strange animal noises again. She'd gotten a B+ on a math test. Her father had taken her to a miniature golf course. Luke and Travis were teaching her to skateboard, or trying to anyway. She didn't think she'd ever master a single trick. She'd let Grace and Hannah give her a mani-pedi and was considering the full makeover they wanted to do. A bad cold was going around the school, so she was drinking lots of orange juice to ward it off, so far with success.

Her life sounded wonderful.

She'd asked questions, too, about Crow and how he spent his days, what he was studying and what he was doing. She asked whether he'd learned anything new about how he died, and whether he knew any magical creatures besides himself. Her mother used to tell her about vampires, werewolves, and other monsters, and she thought he might have met some of them.

Crow's response sat on his desk. Delivery was proving difficult. Mrs. Darlingson—who must not have bought Crow's botched-science-experiment story after all—had installed a dead bolt on Crow's door, and it locked from the hallway. Bars secured the window, imprisoning Crow inside his bedroom.

"What if there's a fire?" he asked. Already dead, he was invulnerable to many things, but fire was not among them. And he hadn't really meant what he'd said before, that his parents shouldn't have brought

68

him back. What he had wasn't much, but it was better than nothing.

"That's very unlikely," Mrs. Darlingson said. "But if there is a fire, the alarms will go off, and I'll open your door. Don't worry."

Instead of replacing the wire, Mrs. Darlingson had gotten rid of the phone. Now the only phone in the house was her cell, which she kept with her at all times. Crow still had his computer, but it had been moved to the living room, where Mrs. Darlingson monitored its use.

He found no more letters from Melody. She was still writing them, he believed. He had to believe that. But his mother kept them far away from him.

Saturday morning, Crow stared at the street from his barred window. His father was visiting. He'd bring a gift—he always did—and for at least a few hours, Crow wouldn't feel like a prisoner. For the first time in days, he smiled.

"Why don't you read something?" Mrs. Darlingson suggested.

"But Dad'll be here any minute."

"No. Not today." She closed the blinds. "With everything that's been going on, I didn't think this was the best time for a visit. I told him not to come."

"But I need to talk to him," Crow said. Although he supposed that was the problem, wasn't it? She must have realized he would ask his father about the Meera. That was why she didn't want him visiting.

"The two of us will still have fun," Mrs. Darlingson said. "Why don't we play Scrabble?"

Even after it had become clear that Crow was no longer a normal, healthy boy, Mr. Darlingson had continued trying to make things as normal as possible. A couple of days after the bowling incident, he came into the living room with a ball and glove. "Let's play baseball in the backyard."

"I don't think that's a good idea," Mrs. Darlingson said. "Why don't you stay inside instead?"

But Mr. Darlingson put his foot down. "A boy can't be cooped up on such a nice day. Crow, get your bat."

Crow, who had eaten nothing but a few nibbles of cracker since the bowling night, had a stomach-ache. Every inch of him hurt, for his nerves had not yet dulled. He didn't want to disappoint his father, though, and he had been wanting to improve his batting, so he went outside without protest.

The sun beamed down, but no one said anything about the growing stench.

Mr. Darlingson pitched the ball. Crow swung and missed.

"That's okay," Mr. Darlingson said, and they tried again. And again, and again, and again, as the sun crept toward the horizon. Crow had known that he needed practice, but he'd never been this bad before. It must have been his arms, which ached so badly he could barely think.

"Are you feeling all right, Crow?"

Crow nodded, despite noticing that his stomach had grown tender and slightly swollen. He prepared to try to hit the ball again. Then he collapsed onto the ground.

Mr. Darlingson ran to his side. "It's okay, Crow. I'm here. It's okay."

A maggot, the first of many, crawled out of Crow's mouth, but Mr. Darlingson kept assuring his son that everything was fine.

But now Crow knew that it had been a lie. Nothing would ever be okay again.

The doorbell rang.

Crow put down his copy of *Gulliver's Travels,* which he wasn't enjoying anyway. All the exciting adventures made him feel even worse about being trapped inside his house. He raced downstairs.

Mrs. Darlingson was dousing the living room in air freshener.

"Aren't you going to answer the door?" Crow demanded, but before his mother could respond, the doorknob started to turn. Crow's smile grew so big that his dry lips started to tear, but he didn't care. Other than his mother, only one person had a key.

The front door opened, and Mr. Darlingson stepped inside.

"Mom said you weren't coming." Crow ran forward to hug his father.

Mr. Darlingson placed a large rectangular box in Crow's outstretched hands. "I thought we needed some father-son time."

Crow got a pair of scissors from the kitchen and opened the box. "An air hockey table!" They used to play air hockey at the arcade all the time—before Crow had died, of course.

"You can't play that in my living room," Mrs. Darlingson said.

"And you can't tell me not to see my son," Mr. Darlingson snapped. "Relax. It's a mini air hockey table. It's supposed to be played indoors. Go ahead, Crow. Set it up."

Crow shot his mother a nervous glance, but she'd returned to her dusting. With his father's help, he set up the game on the coffee table, where they had to kneel to play.

"Goal!" Crow yelled. "Five to three." He suspected his father was going easy on him, but it was still fun.

"No yelling in the house," Mrs. Darlingson scolded.

"Then where is he supposed to yell?" asked Mr. Darlingson. "If the noise is bothering you, you can go upstairs, you know."

Mrs. Darlingson stayed where she was.

Mr. Darlingson started the next round. Crow tried to focus. If he played better, his father wouldn't have to let him win. He hit the puck as hard as he could. Too hard. It ricocheted off the table and hit the television.

"I told you it was a bad idea to play that here!" Mrs. Darlingson said. "Now look what you've done."

"We haven't done anything. The television's fine." Mr. Darlingson retrieved the puck. "Let's play some more."

"No," Mrs. Darlingson said. "That's enough."

Crow sensed that a fight was about to start—a real fight, one that would make the present bickering look peaceful in comparison. "It's okay. We can take a break. Let's go up to my room so I can show you some drawings I'm working on." Actually, he wanted to talk, but he didn't want to give his mother a reason to eavesdrop.

Crow and Mr. Darlingson went upstairs. Mrs. Darlingson stayed downstairs. Perfect.

"I want to know more about the Meera," Crow said as soon as he'd shut the door.

"Why are there bars on your window?"

"What? Oh, Mom put them there. She put a lock on my door, too. But about the Meera—"

Mr. Darlingson examined the locks. "She's trapping you in here? That's it. Stay here." He stormed downstairs.

A shouting match quickly followed.

"You can't treat him like this!"

"I'm protecting him!"

"By locking him inside? You've gone too far. I'm tempted to report you."

"You wouldn't dare. You know what would happen to him if people found out."

"Could it be worse than this? His room might as well be a prison. You have no right."

Crow couldn't listen anymore. They were arguing, and even worse, it was about him. They'd talked about getting a divorce before Crow died, but then he came back and things seemed better for a while. He couldn't help wondering if they would have worked things out if he hadn't started to rot and stink.

He wanted things to go back to the way they had been. Maybe one day, his wish would be granted. In the meantime, he turned on some music—his mother hadn't taken that away—and tried to drown out the noise.

Despite his parents' fight, nothing changed. By the time Halloween arrived, Crow still hadn't managed to get a message to Melody. His father's words echoed in his ears. His mother had no right to keep him trapped like this.

The guest bedroom hadn't been used in years, which meant no one would miss the sheets. Crow took one, plain white, off the bed. He cut out two small holes. He trimmed the bottom so he wouldn't trip and draped it over himself. With an empty pillowcase in hand, he was set.

Mrs. Darlingson stopped him at the door. "Where do you think you're going? And what have you done to my sheet?"

"I'm a ghost," he said. "You promised me I could go trick-or-treating."

"That was before you started sneaking out at night. You didn't really think I'd still let you go, did you?"

Honestly, no, he didn't. The fact that she hadn't sewn a costume for him made it pretty clear. But that wasn't going to stop him. He couldn't spend one more night alone in his room, much less the eternity his mother seemed set on.

He opened the front door. The bells his mother had put there clattered noisily. "You promised."

"Come here right now!"

"Or what? You'll ground me? I don't have anything left for you to take away. Dad was right. You can't do this. Maybe I would be happier living with him." Except, of course, his father hadn't offered. His small apartment wasn't designed for two people, especially not when one of them stank. But that was beside the point right now. "Make that definitely. I hate living with you."

"How can you say that?" Her voice had softened. She looked really hurt.

Crow felt bad—but not bad enough to stop. "I just want to go trick-or-treating. I'll be back in a few hours."

He stepped outside and shut the door behind him. To his surprise, it stayed shut. Mrs. Darlingson didn't chase after him and drag him inside. She didn't yell at him from the living room. Of course, she'd have plenty to say to him later, but there was no point in thinking about that now. He had a holiday to enjoy.

It was early—not even five o'clock yet. Hopefully Melody was still home. He walked over and rang the doorbell.

Mr. Plympton answered, dressed as a chicken and holding a big bowl of candy.

"Is Melody here?" Crow asked. "We're supposed to go trick-or-treating together."

"I thought she was going with Grace and Hannah." Mr. Plympton moved his head around, searching for an angle that would let him peer into the eyeholes in Crow's sheet. "Who are you? Luke? Or is it Travis?"

The Plymptons' dog, a floppy-eared mutt, sniffed Crow a couple of times before it started growling.

"Travis," Crow said, remembering what Mr. Plympton had said before. He didn't want his daughter spending time with a boy whose flesh rotted off. Okay, that wasn't exactly what he had said, but Crow was sure it was what he had meant. "The five of us are going together," he added.

"She's putting on her costume. Why don't you wait inside?"

"No thanks. I'll wait out here." In a warm and enclosed space, the stench would be more noticeable. A lot more noticeable. Crow couldn't risk it. Besides, the dog was still growling at him.

"Suit yourself." Mr. Plympton shut the door.

Crow examined the Plymptons' Halloween decorations, an elaborate graveyard scene, before sitting down between an inflatable vampire and a plastic tombstone. The seconds ticked by. The minutes crawled past. He wondered if Melody was avoiding him. Maybe she was mad because he hadn't responded to any of her letters.

The front door opened. Crow jumped up.

"What are you doing here?" Melody demanded. "Why don't you guys just leave me alone?"

Crow's entire body slumped. "I'm sorry. I won't bother you anymore." He started to walk away, ready to go back home and apologize to his mother. "Wait . . . what do you mean *you guys*?"

"Crow?" Melody whispered. "Crow, is that you?"

He nodded underneath his sheet.

She sniffed the air a few times. Her nose scrunched up, but then she smiled. "It *is* you! My dad said you were Travis."

"So you're not mad at me?"

Her eyes widened. "Of course I'm not mad! I thought you were mad at me. Didn't you get my letters? Or my

77

emails? Or my phone messages? I called you like a billion times."

"My mom cut the telephone wire. She hid the letters from me, too, and then when I found them, I think she started throwing them away." He frowned. "And I guess she blocked your emails. I didn't know about those until just now."

"Oh. Sorry I couldn't visit you at night anymore, but my dad had a fit." She smiled. "I like your costume. It's funny, you know, 'cause you're dead."

"I like your costume, too. You look . . ." He paused. If his blood had still circulated, he would have blushed. "Nice."

"I'm supposed to look scary," she said.

Crow frowned. She was wearing large purple and pink wings, a blue leotard, and antennae. "What's scary about a butterfly?"

"They're just fancy moths, and everyone hates those. A cousin of mine had a moth crawl into her ear once. She had to go to the hospital to have it removed, and I think it ate some of her brain before the doctors could get it out. That's why she's so stupid. See?" She pointed to some red smeared around her mouth. "Fake blood. I'm a brain-eating butterfly."

Crow was pretty sure butterflies didn't eat brains, and neither did moths, but he decided not to say anything about it.

"I'll be back in one second. Wait here." Melody ran inside her house.

A couple of minutes later, she returned, and although she didn't say anything about what she had needed, Crow couldn't help noticing a bit of gloss under her nostrils. She'd gone inside to apply rose oil to her nose so the smell wouldn't bother her. Crow didn't mind. Well, he may have minded, but he understood.

"Do you need to find Grace and Hannah?" he asked. "And Luke and Travis? Your dad said you were trick-or-treating with them." Even though he had made plans with Melody first. But he supposed a bigger group would be okay, as long as the other kids didn't mind the smell. Maybe he could say it was part of his costume.

"Not anymore. We got into a fight." She started walking to the neighbor's house. "Come on. We won't get any candy standing here."

The first house gave them two miniature candy bars each. The second house gave them rather old-looking lollipops, which was still better than the third house, where they received toothpaste. At the fourth house, a large zombie appeared suddenly, causing Melody to laugh and Crow to scream. The zombie—a person in costume, Crow realized—gave them loads of chocolate.

Too bad Crow couldn't eat any of it. Oh well, he'd

give it all to Melody. If she got twice as much candy, she'd definitely want to go trick-or-treating with him again the next year.

They were walking to the next block when Melody suddenly stopped. Her bag of candy slipped from her hands. Without bothering to pick up the bag, she ran behind a parked car.

Crow picked up the bag.

Melody had seen something. Something scary.

And what was scarier than the Meera? Crow left his house on Halloween, confident that his disguise could hide him. Maybe the Meera had picked the holiday to wander the streets, too.

Crow crouched behind the car with Melody.

CHAPTER NINE

The street lamps flickered on. Crow searched the shadows and listened to the breeze. If the Meera was anywhere nearby, it was hiding itself very well. Aside from the other trick-or-treaters, Crow couldn't see or hear anything.

"Why are we hiding?" he whispered.

Melody nodded toward a pair of girls. "Grace and Hannah. I don't want them to see me."

Hannah was dressed as a princess, which Crow guessed was meant to remind everyone that she was related to royalty. Or claimed to be, anyway. Her tiara sparkled under the street lamps. Grace wore a Greek goddess dress with matching earrings and an armband. They were as cute as ever, although he thought they were wearing a little too much makeup, even if it was Halloween. He didn't see how the high heels would make trick-or-treating any easier, either. And he knew for a fact that the ancient Greeks didn't wear shoes like that. Grace could have chosen something a little more historically accurate.

They didn't look scary, though. They certainly didn't look like anything people needed to hide from.

"Why can't they see you?"

"I told you. We're in a fight." Her body slumped. Her hands covered her face. "It was awful."

Crow waited a moment. When she didn't say anything, and she didn't look any happier, he asked, "What happened?"

"I was just explaining to Luke and Travis why I think the school librarian is an alien. We're so close to Area Fifty-One, and she has this weird thing on the back of her neck that I'm pretty sure is a second mouth, probably the one she uses to eat people. At first, they seemed really interested in my theory, asking for more details and stuff. I thought someone finally believed me! But then they started making fun of me."

"Oh." He looked at Grace and Hannah. "What about them?"

"They were supposed to be my friends, so I thought they'd back me up. But when I told them, they made fun of me, too. And then they told everyone! Now the entire school thinks I'm crazy." She brought her hands down from her face and crossed them. "I don't care. I don't even need any friends—except you, of course. You'd never be mean to me. You can be my best friend!"

Crow couldn't help smiling. She wanted him to be her best friend. Not just a friend—her *best* friend. Thankfully, the sheet masked his joy, which seemed horribly inappropriate considering how upset Melody was.

He wanted to say something, but he wasn't used to comforting people. His hand jerked a few times as he debated whether he should hug her. That was what the people on television always did. Then the maggots started squirming, and this convinced him to keep his putrid hands to himself.

They sat in silence, watching Grace and Hannah. Hannah stopped to fix her tiara. Grace ate a piece of chocolate. She threw the wrapper on the ground. A moment later, they disappeared around a corner.

"You're lucky," Melody said as they walked toward the next house. "You don't have to go to school."

"I want to go to school. It's better than staying home alone all day."

Melody winced. "Of course. I'm sorry. Um, how did your parents wish you back to life? I know I've asked you before, and I guess you don't like talking about it, but—"

"It's okay," Crow interrupted. "They went to the Meera—that's the monster we heard at the park—and wished for me to come back." Not wanting her to think that he'd withheld information earlier, he quickly added, "I just found that out recently, after our trip to the park."

Melody blinked several times. She opened her mouth, closed it, and blinked some more. "There's a monster at the park, and it grants wishes? That's great! I knew what we heard that night couldn't have been a regular animal, so I kept going back, but I couldn't find anything. Maybe you can wish for a normal life!"

"Yeah. Maybe." But that would mean returning to the park. Facing the monster. It hadn't gone so well last time, and he had the singed hair to prove it.

They'd reached the next house. Crow rang the doorbell, and he and Melody received some chocolate. Then he hurried on to the next house, hoping Melody would be too busy running after him to remember what they had been talking about.

More chocolate. Some lollipops. Some gum. Raisins. Caramels. They moved on to the next block.

"Oh no!" Melody whispered. She was staring at two boys, one dressed as a cowboy, the other as a pirate, both standing in the middle of the street. Crow recognized the cowboy as Luke, which made the pirate Travis.

"Do we need to hide again?" he asked.

"No. Just ignore them."

They continued walking, heads held high and eyes focused straight ahead. A car honked, but neither of them looked to see why. A series of loud noises followed, short banging sounds that made Crow jump. Curiosity got the better of him. He stopped walking and looked at the source of the noise.

Travis was holding a lighter in one hand and a small item in the other. He lit the item and threw it at the ground, where it exploded with a deafening crack.

Melody groaned. "They've been bragging about those stupid firecrackers all week. I don't know why. They're not nearly as impressive as fireworks."

The driver of a red truck blocked by the boys certainly wasn't impressed. He honked his horn again, but Luke and Travis stayed where they were. The driver went around them slowly. Luke threw a firecracker at the truck as it passed.

Melody tugged at Crow's sheet. "Let's get out of here."

"Wait," Crow said.

A group of boys was crossing the street several yards away. They were young, probably in third or fourth grade, and Luke and Travis were headed straight for them.

Travis snatched a bag of candy from a small boy in a superhero costume.

"Give that back!" the boy yelled. His friends hurried across the street, leaving him to fend for himself.

Luke and Travis passed the stolen loot back and forth, always keeping it inches beyond the reach of the younger boy, who seemed on the verge of tears. His friends cowered in the background.

Earlier, Melody had been like that little boy. No one had stood up for her, either.

Crow couldn't watch anymore. He marched over to Luke. "Give him back his candy."

"Why would I do that?" Luke smirked under his cowboy hat. "Nice costume. Did your mommy make it for you?"

"No. I made it myself. Give him his candy."

"Why don't you give it to him?" He threw the bag to Travis. "You just have to get it from us first."

"I can't reach," Crow said to Travis. "You're at least a foot taller than me."

Travis smiled as if this were something to be proud of. As if either of them had any control over their height.

Luke and Travis weren't just taller than Crow. They could jump higher and run faster, too. Crow would never succeed in taking the bag from them. Instead of making a pathetic attempt, he handed his own bag to the small boy in the superhero costume. "Here, you can have mine. Sorry, it's not much."

The little boy just stared at him.

"It's okay, really. I can't eat candy anyway."

The boy took the bag and ran off to his friends.

"Come on, Crow," Melody whispered. Her eyes

darted back and forth between Luke and Travis. "Let's go."

"Look, Travis," Luke said. "It's Smelody. I saw an alien a few houses down. It wants us to think it's just a kid in a costume, but you know better."

"Shut up, Luke."

Luke pretended to look shocked. "Shut up? Me? Melodork, I thought we were friends." He lit a firecracker and threw it. "Guess not."

The first firecracker was followed by a second from Travis, then a third and a fourth. Crow couldn't tell whether they were actually aiming for him and Melody, but the firecrackers were getting awfully close regardless. "Come on, Melody. You were right. We should go."

"Crow!" Melody screamed. "Your sheet's on fire!"

Crow glanced over his shoulder and saw the flames crawling up his back. There was little pain—his nerves had decayed like everything else—but that wouldn't stop his flesh from burning. He scrambled to remove the sheet.

"Why—What—" Travis squinted at Crow in the light of the street lamps and of the burning sheet. Apparently still unsure of what he was seeing, he removed his eye patch to get a better look. "Why are you wearing a costume under your costume?"

A maggot crawled out of Crow's ear.

"What is *that*?" Luke asked, stepping forward to investigate. Crow scurried away, tripping over the curb in his rush. His chin smacked against the pavement, the jolt causing his left eye to pop out of the socket. It rolled into the path of some trick-or-treaters, who were too busy staring at the burning sheet to notice. A pink ballet slipper hovered over the eye, an eye that Crow could still see through. He watched in horror as the shoe stomped down.

CHAPTER TEN

Melody shoved the ballerina. While the ballerina's friends helped her up, Melody snatched the runaway eyeball.

Travis and Luke had already fled. Crow was thankful they were gone, even though it didn't seem fair. Stealing, lighting firecrackers, setting someone on fire—were they really going to get away with it all?

A man carrying a fire extinguisher approached the burning sheet. "Move out of the way," he ordered the kids who had gathered around to watch the flames. He released a stream of white foam that doused the fire.

The man returned to his house, leaving the sheet behind. The crowd of onlookers dispersed.

Crow prodded his sheet with his foot. The remaining scraps of charred material wouldn't be enough to cover him.

"It's okay," Melody said, stepping onto the sidewalk as a silver sedan approached. "You don't need the sheet."

Crow nodded and followed her, but the empty eye socket was already drawing a lot of attention. A group of little children screamed when they saw him. A mother herded her daughters to the other side of the street. A toddler started crying. Even on Halloween, he couldn't pass for normal.

Melody held on to the eye. The split vision that resulted—the lines of Melody's palm with one eye, and the dark street with the other—made Crow dizzy. He stumbled into a bush. He barreled into a family dressed as assorted fruit. A car nearly ran him over when he lurched into the street.

"Where are we going?" he asked.

"We need to wash off the eye, right? And then, I don't know, do we just pop it back in?"

Crow nodded. "I don't think we even need to wash it first. Infection isn't really a problem for me."

"Of course we need to wash it. It's covered in dirt." She peeled off a candy wrapper that had been stuck to the white of the eye. "And viruses might not be a problem for you, but what about parasites? And fungus? I read an article about a brain-eating fungus that keeps popping up all over the country. Brain-eating. Even you would be hurt by that. We need to wash the eye off."

"Okay. Where?"

"The park."

Crow walked into a telephone pole. "What? Why there?" He wanted to face the Meera again, but not so soon. Not without a plan. And definitely not tonight, when it was already so dark.

"Where else?" Melody asked. "I don't want to risk going home—what if Grace and Hannah have stopped by, and my dad realized I wasn't with them? And I think he'd freak out if he saw your eye. We could go to your house, but I don't think your mom likes me very much. The park has a water fountain we can use, with no parents to bother us."

"It's not personal. My mom doesn't like anyone." He paused for a moment, thinking. Nothing in the park would pose much of a threat as long as they stayed away from the storage shed. "You're right. We should go to the park."

"And while we're there," Melody added, running ahead of him, "maybe we can get the Meera to grant you a wish."

The water dripped brown and foul-smelling from the fountain.

"Maybe we should go somewhere else," Melody said.

"No. This is good enough." Crow rinsed the eyeball off before shoving it back into his socket.

"Can you see all right?"

He blinked a few times, and the two streams of vision synced up. "Yeah, I can see fine. Do you want to trick-or-treat some more?" Maybe she'd forget about the Meera.

Before she could answer, a cracking sound pierced the night.

Crack! Crack! Crack!

It was a familiar noise, one that Crow had heard only minutes earlier. With his eyes working properly again, he could see its source, too. Luke and Travis.

Grace and Hannah were with them.

Melody hid behind a tree. "Come here. Don't let them see you."

"One second," Crow said, his curiosity getting the better of him. He thought he had seen something in the flash of explosions.

While Grace and Hannah cheered them on, Luke and Travis threw their firecrackers. But they didn't throw them randomly; they were throwing them at something. Crow inched closer to see what exactly that something was.

The explosions cast an unsteady light on a pair of long ears and a twitching nose. A rabbit. The poor thing looked terrified.

But was it really scared? Was it even a rabbit? Crow

doubted anything so helpless could live next to a monster.

And the monster could take on any form it pleased, small or large, terrified or terrifying.

"Leave it alone!" Crow yelled.

"You again?" Travis threw a firecracker at Crow. "Freak! Want to be set on fire again?"

Crow dodged the firecracker. "I think you should leave that rabbit alone. I think it's dangerous."

"Dangerous? A rabbit! What's it going to do? Nuzzle me to death? Or is it supposed to be an alien, too?" Luke threw another firecracker so that it landed right next to the animal.

The rabbit growled.

Grace and Hannah, who had been laughing the entire time, fell silent. Luke and Travis stopped throwing firecrackers. One, already lit, burned Luke's hand. He dropped it, not really paying attention, and it exploded at his feet.

The rabbit had transformed.

It had the lower body and eyes of a goat, the claws and tail of a scorpion, and the beak and wings of an owl. A single horn, long and sharp, rose from the center of its forehead. A silver collar engraved with a series of spiraling symbols, like some unknown language, wrapped around its neck. Its skin was a complex tapestry of fur, feathers, and scales.

This was the Meera's true form. This was what had stood over Crow's casket years ago.

Spiderwebs shot out from the Meera's torso. The sticky silk covered Luke, who struggled unsuccessfully to break free. When the Meera tugged at the webbing, Luke fell. His screams filled the park.

Grace and Hannah picked up stones to throw at the Meera. It snarled in response. A second stream of spiderweb flew toward them.

Travis yanked on their arms, pulling them out of the way just in time to avoid being trapped in the webbing. The three of them fled while the monster dragged their friend into the storage shed.

Luke's screams faded. The park was silent once more.

"What do we do now?" Melody asked.

Crow walked toward the shed. "We follow him."

CHAPTER ELEVEN

Before crawling through the hole left by the missing panel, Melody removed a flashlight from her trick-or-treat bag and turned it on. Once inside, the light revealed Luke's Halloween bag, the candy spilling out onto the filthy floor, but no sign of Luke himself.

"Where did he go?" she asked.

Crow shrugged. Without furniture or supplies, the room offered no hiding spots. But the Meera had definitely entered the shed, dragging Luke behind it, so he had to be there somewhere.

Melody shined her light on the ceiling. Thick tangles of spiderweb covered every inch, but there was no boy trapped inside.

Something buzzed in the corner of the shed. Crow elbowed Melody and pointed to where he wanted the light. A fly, no bigger than the yellowed fingernail on Crow's pinkie, flew around for a minute before landing on the wall.

"What did you do with Luke?" Crow asked the fly.

The fly ignored him.

"I know you're the Meera." Actually, he knew no such thing. It could have been a common housefly that just happened to wander into the shed. But he suspected otherwise. "Tell me where Luke is."

The fly grew fur, a tail, claws, and teeth. Mostly, it just grew.

Definitely the Meera.

Crow tried to stand his ground, but his knees wobbled. "Wh-where's Luke?"

The Meera, now in the shape of a lion, roared. Its sharp teeth glistened in the glow of the flashlight. Crow had liked it better as a rabbit.

"Maybe we should go," Melody whispered.

"What about Luke? And what about the wish?" If he left now, he doubted he'd ever work up the courage to come back. "You can go if you want. But can you give me your flashlight?" He held out his hand.

"No. I'll stay if you stay." The light shook in her trembling grasp. "Can't run away from a mystery, can I?"

The lion roared again, its breath hot on Crow's skin. He was sure the beast was about to eat him, but he couldn't remember how to move. So he stood there, perfectly still, while the lion's mouth opened wide and enveloped his head. Its teeth scraped against his scalp. Its tongue dripped saliva onto his nose. Everything was dark and hot and moist.

"Where is Luke?" he asked, his voice echoing in the large cavern of the lion's mouth. "And h-how do I get a wish?"

The lion roared, but it didn't chomp down. Crow took that as a good sign.

"I know you grant wishes. My parents came to you a few years ago. You brought me back from the dead, but not completely. So now I need to make it right. I need a wish."

Another roar, but still no chewing.

"There's a test, right? I'm ready for it."

The lion stepped back, releasing Crow's head from its mouth. Its mane disappeared. Its golden fur transformed into a tabby pattern, and it shrank into a fluffy, wide-eyed kitten.

Adorable, Crow thought, though he felt no urge to pet it.

The kitten walked to a metal grate in the floor. It pawed at the grate, meowing.

"Are we supposed to go through there?" Melody asked.

"I think so." Crow wedged his fingers into a gap between the concrete ground and the metal grate. The grate lifted easily. Melody shined her flashlight down the large hole it left. It was a six-foot drop, give or take a foot.

Crow jumped, once again thankful that his mother had reinforced his joints. He looked around, but without the flashlight, all he could see was an impenetrable blanket of darkness.

Above, the kitten meowed. Then it roared, and Melody jumped.

"You didn't say anything about a test," she said, rubbing her ankle.

"I didn't think we'd be taking it tonight. Are you okay?"

"Yeah." She stood up straight. "What do we do now?"

She turned around slowly, letting her flashlight reveal their surroundings. They were in a long, narrow tunnel. In one direction, the tunnel ended just a few feet away. In the other direction, it went on farther than the flashlight could show. The walls were packed earth, decorated with a series of identical engravings, each depicting a tortoise. There were torches, too, but they were unlit. Melody's flashlight provided the only light.

"I guess we walk."

She nodded, and they started forward.

"I'm not surprised, you know," she said.

"Oh," Crow said. "About what?"

"This." She gestured around the tunnel with her

flashlight. "The monster. The secret passageway under the park. All of it. This sort of thing is more common than most people want to believe. My old town had monsters, too. Nobody believed it, of course, not even with all the strange stuff that kept happening. Weather changed without warning. Adults got mad for no reason. Sometimes they even slurred their speech, wobbled around, and talked nonsense, all clear signs of mass possession. Some people knew, I'm pretty sure, but they kept everything hush. A real conspiracy."

"Oh," Crow said, not sure whether sudden rainstorms or short tempers were all that strange. Not compared to their current situation.

A long howl echoed through the tunnel, followed by a scream that sounded very human. Crow couldn't tell if it came from behind them or ahead of them. Close or far away.

"Is that Luke?" Melody asked.

"Who else could it be?"

When the howling and the screaming faded, they walked in silence.

Crow kept expecting the tunnel to end, or to open into a room, or to turn, or to do *something*, but instead it just went on and on. After a while, he started counting the tortoise engravings. Five. Thirty-three. Seventy-eight. Three hundred, and still no end in sight.

"Let's take a break," Melody said. She sat down on

the ground and opened her trick-or-treat bag. While she ate some chocolate, Crow examined one of the engravings. The tortoise had a foot stretched out, like it was walking, just like the other 299 engravings they'd passed.

"What kind of test do we have to take?" Melody asked.

Crow sat next to her. "I don't know. My dad never said."

"I hope it's not math. I've never been any good at math. Or history. Maybe we'll get lucky and I'll get a juggling test and you'll get a drawing test. Then we're sure to pass." She hesitated. "What happens if we fail?"

"I'm not sure. Not exactly. Some sort of punishment." Or death, but Crow didn't want to scare her any more than was necessary. "We should definitely make sure we don't fail."

"And if we pass, we get a wish?"

Crow nodded.

"Well, I know what you're going to wish for." She stood up. "But neither of us will ever get a wish if we don't get out of this tunnel and start the test. Maybe we should head back. We might have missed a secret door or something. Or we could ask the Mar . . . Mor . . ."

"Meera."

"Or we could ask the Meera for instructions." She

shined her light the way they had come, squinting into the darkness. "That's strange."

She ran a few paces, retracing their steps, and Crow ran with her. Then suddenly they both stopped. They had to. There was nothing but solid wall in front of them; the tunnel had ended.

Melody shined her light at the ceiling. There was a metal grate, exactly like the one they'd come through. "We're where we started again. But how is that possible? We walked for a long time—miles, I think—but after we turned around, we only ran a few feet." She frowned. "Maybe the tunnel looped?"

Crow shook his head. "The tunnel's straight. And if it were a loop, it would go on in both directions. Give me a piece of your chocolate."

Melody handed the candy to him. "I thought you couldn't eat."

"I can't." He unwrapped the chocolate and smeared it against the ground. It wasn't quite as good as chalk, but it would have to do. He drew an arrow. "Let's start walking again. I want to test something."

They resumed walking. A couple of minutes later, they passed the arrow. A couple of minutes after that, they passed it again.

Crow pointed to the arrow the third time they passed it. "We keep traveling the same stretch of hallway, again and again and again."

"So it's magic." She smiled. "Even before I met you, I knew magic was real. Ever since I found a fairy circle as a child. Sure, my dad said it was just a bunch of ordinary mushrooms, but then why would they have been growing in a perfect circle?"

Crow was about to explain that the mushroom circle was simply the visible part of an underground fungus and not evidence of fairy habitation, but he stopped himself. Maybe Melody was right, and magic was responsible. As an animated corpse, standing in a strange tunnel guarded by an even stranger wish-granting shape-shifter, he felt unqualified to argue against magic.

"Should we go back up?" Melody asked. She pointed to the grate that, despite all the walking they'd done, was only a short distance away. "You can give me a boost, and then I'll help pull you up."

Another howl made her last words difficult to hear. There was more screaming, too.

"No," Crow said. "I think we need to keep walking."

Melody frowned. "But the tunnel doesn't go any-where. We could walk forever and end up right where we started."

Crow walked over to the nearest engraving. "The tortoise is walking. It's a sign. A hint. We have to walk, too. This is the test."

"Are you sure?"

No. "Yes. Mostly. And if I'm wrong, what's the worst that could happen?"

"We could spend days down here. Our parents could call the police to file a missing-child report. We could die of dehydration. Well, I could die." She looked at the tortoise. "But I think you're right. And I do want a wish. And to find out more about this Meera."

They kept walking. Time passed, but it was impossible to say how much.

At first, nothing changed, but then the floor became muddy. As their feet sank farther and farther into the thick sludge, every step became a struggle. Soon it came up to their ankles, then their knees. When it reached their hips, Crow wondered whether they would get stuck. He tried to swim, thinking that if he could float up to the top, the mud wouldn't be so bad, but his feet always sank to the bottom. Melody's efforts met with no more success.

Now the sludge reached their shoulders. Melody held the flashlight and her bag of candy above her head.

The tortoise engravings urged them on, but the tortoise didn't have mud up to its chin. Any higher, and Melody would suffocate. And even with the greatest effort, Crow moved only a fraction of an inch. He would get stuck there, he feared. Stuck for eternity. He wouldn't even be able to die, since he had already done that.

He wanted to turn back, to return to the safety of his house. But turning back would mean failure, and he still didn't know what happened to those who failed. Perhaps something even worse than getting stuck in mud. He forced himself forward, one tiny step at a time.

Melody coughed, spitting out the mud that had seeped into her mouth.

"Give me your stuff," Crow said, worried that she'd drop everything. He took the candy and the flashlight and held them as high as he could above the muck.

Melody took another step, then another, then another, even as the mud covered her nose. She closed her eyes as the mud crept up to her forehead. Every now and then, she jumped up in an attempt to reach air.

Just a few steps behind her, Crow did his best to continue forward. He imagined that Melody's head became completely submerged, but he couldn't be certain. Thick sludge now covered his eyes, too, and even when he forced them open, he couldn't see anything. One of his hands kept the flashlight and candy held above his head, but it was only a matter of time before the mud covered everything.

They would be buried alive. Melody would, anyway. Crow would just be buried. It was actually kind of fitting, not that this made him feel any better about the situation.

He stopped. Clearly they had lost, so what was the point in struggling anymore?

Something reached through the mud and touched Crow's free hand. He recoiled, fearful of the creatures that might hide in the Meera's lair, but the thing persisted. Fingers wrapped around fingers. It was Melody's hand. She was pulling him forward.

The mud levels receded. Crow wiped the mud from his eyes, and they scrambled onto solid ground, Melody gasping for air. The test was over. They had passed.

CHAPTER TWELVE

Water spurted from the top of a large, two-tiered fountain located in the center of a dark room.

"Do you think it's safe?" Melody asked.

"Is anything safe here? But I don't think the Meera would mess with the water. It wants to test us, not poison us."

Crow and Melody clambered onto the lower level, where they washed away the mud. Once they were clean enough to move without the muck weighing them down, Melody gulped water from the upper level, while Crow used the flashlight to examine their new surroundings.

The tunnel had disappeared. Now there was only a single room, about the size of Crow's bedroom except with a much higher ceiling. The walls were natural dirt again, lacking both windows and doors. Just like in the tunnel, unlit torches and a series of engravings decorated the walls, although the familiar tortoise was nowhere to be seen. The engravings here depicted a bird.

In addition to the fountain—which looked suspiciously similar to an oversized birdbath—there was a long, thick coil of rope and a large pile of sticks left in a heap on the ground.

Melody, soaked and shivering, climbed down from the fountain. "What now?"

"I think this is the second test, but I'm not sure what we're supposed to do. There doesn't seem to be a way out."

"What about up there?" Melody pointed toward the ceiling. "I think I saw something while I was getting a drink."

Crow shined the flashlight up where she had pointed. Sure enough, there was an opening in the wall, just big enough to crawl through and about twenty feet above his head. "How are we supposed to reach it?"

She shook her head and shrugged. "No idea."

Crow sat down. This was a test, which meant there had to be a way to pass. He just needed to figure out what the Meera wanted them to do. In the last test, the engraved tortoise had urged them to keep walking.

"Does the bird mean we're supposed to fly?" he asked, shining the flashlight on the new engravings.

"I hope not." She took off her butterfly wings, the flimsy material now a torn and tattered mess. "You don't think the Meera thought these were real, do you?"

"No. I don't know. Maybe. But they're not, so we'd better find another way up." He stood. The wall had a series of small holes, each about an inch and a half in diameter and half a foot deep, leading up to the larger hole that hopefully provided an exit. After handing the flashlight back to Melody, he reached his fingers into one of the small holes. Then he did the same with his other hand and another hole. But when he tried to pull himself up, his fingers failed to support his weight. He couldn't get his feet off the ground, and if he kept trying, he worried his fingers would tear off, even though they had been reinforced with stitches.

"These holes are too small. I can't get a good grip."

"What about that hook?" Melody shined the light at a metal hook positioned above the larger hole. "Maybe we're supposed to use that."

"The rope!" Crow ran over to the length of rope. "We can tie a loop at one end, throw it over the hook, and use the rope to climb up."

He'd studied knots a while ago and had gotten very good at tying the double overhand, the alpine butterfly, and the anchor hitch, among others. A figure eight follow-through struck him as best suited for the task, so he got to work on the complicated twists.

Unfortunately, tying knots in shoelaces had been

somewhat easier than tying knots in thick rope proved to be, and a few fuzzy spots in Crow's memory necessitated some trial and error. He looped and unlooped, tied and untied, until finally he had a knot strong enough to hold the weight of two eleven-year-olds. Hopefully. Just to be sure, he'd climb up ahead of Melody.

But before either of them could start climbing, they had to get the knot around the hook. Crow tossed it up. It didn't even make it halfway before gravity pulled it down. He tried again, this time with all his strength, and failed again.

Melody climbed onto the lower level of the fountain, then the upper level. "Give me the rope. Maybe I can get it from here."

With her first attempt, the rope missed the hook by several feet. With the second attempt, it brushed against the hook. With the fifteenth attempt, she complained about sore arms.

"Keep trying," Crow urged, tossing the fallen rope back to her. "You've almost got it."

"Almost isn't going to help us," she said, but she didn't give up. Eventually, long after Crow had lost count of the attempts, the loop at the end of the rope caught the hook perfectly.

Worried that the rope might break, or that the knot might come undone, he gave it a few good tugs. It seemed secure, so he started to climb.

He made it about six inches off the floor, which left nineteen and a half more feet. Nineteen and a half feet too many. He fell to the floor.

"Let me try," Melody said.

She made it a little over a foot.

"Maybe I'll get farther after a break," she said. "I'm pretty tired."

Crow nodded, although he doubted a break would help any. Neither of them was strong enough to climb a rope all the way to the ceiling, but until he had a better plan, he saw no reason to point this out.

They sat down and leaned against the base of the fountain. Melody selected a lollipop from her bag. "Do you want any candy? I know you said you can't eat, but maybe a piece of gum or something would be okay."

"No thanks. I can't taste anything anymore."

"Okay." She licked her lollipop. "So if your mom has been throwing away my letters, cutting the phone line, and blocking my email, how'd you get her to let you go out tonight?"

"She didn't exactly let me. I just kind of went. Things haven't been great. My dad visited a few days ago, and they got in a big fight about me."

"How long have they been divorced?"

Crow had to count the months, which all seemed to bleed together. "About a year."

"That's not very long. I bet they'll fight less after a while."

"Yeah. I guess. Did your parents get divorced?" He remembered her saying her mother had disappeared and that she blamed magic, but there had to be more to the story.

"No." She took a deep breath. "My mom just sort of vanished. Overnight. I'm pretty sure she was abducted by aliens because I remember seeing strange lights in the sky that night. Or it could have been fairies. They take people sometimes—children, usually, but occasionally adults—and I did find that fairy circle the next day. Some people think fairies and aliens are actually the same thing, so probably both my theories are right."

"What does your dad say happened?"

"That she couldn't handle being a mom. That she walked out on us. But who cares what he says? Obviously he's wrong because magic is real—otherwise we wouldn't be here right now. And Mom wouldn't have just left us. She couldn't have. Fairies took her, or aliens, or something else. Her bedtime stories about monsters had been real all along. She was trying to warn me, but I didn't get it. Not until it was too late."

"That's why you're so interested in magic." His face fell, his shoulders slumped, and he looked down at the dirt ground. "That's why you want to be friends with me."

"Not this again. Listen, when I first met you, I didn't even know you were magical. And maybe I was interested in getting to know you because you were mysterious, but it's not like that now. I think you're nice and fun and smart. After seeing what the kids at school are like, is that really so hard to believe? I'd rather be friends with a maggot." She stood up and marched over to the rope. "Luke doesn't even deserve to be rescued, but I want a wish. I think I'm ready to try again."

She made it about two feet this time. Impressive, but not nearly enough.

"That's a lot farther than I got," Crow said, hoping he sounded encouraging.

Tears welled in Melody's eyes. "Yeah, but it's nowhere near close enough. We're stuck down here."

"No, we're not. This is a test, and we can pass it. My parents passed it, remember? And neither of them can fly, either."

She sniffed. "That's true. Maybe we need to use the sticks."

The sticks! Of course. The Meera wouldn't have left them in the room if they weren't part of the test. Each stick was short, maybe eight inches, and thick enough to be strong—maybe even strong enough to hold their weight, if only they could figure out how to use them.

Melody jumped up. "The holes in the wall!"

She didn't need to say anything else. Crow, understanding at once, grabbed a handful of the sticks and carried them to the spot beneath the exit. He and Melody shoved the sticks into the small holes that lined the wall, creating perfect climbing holds.

Perfect as far as they could reach. Which wasn't very far.

Crow climbed back down. "Give me your trick-or-treat bag. We can put the sticks in it, and I'll carry it up. Can you follow me with the flashlight?"

Melody experimented with different ways of holding the flashlight, finally settling on carrying it in her mouth. When Crow had gathered the rest of the sticks, he followed Melody's lead and held on to the bag by biting a corner.

The first part was easy, but then he ran out of climbing holds. Grabbing on to the rope and keeping his feet on the sticks for support, he climbed a little higher. Then, still hanging on to the rope with one hand, he used his other hand to take a stick from the bag and put it into the next hole.

Up he climbed, inserting one stick at a time, as Melody followed below.

A loud snapping sound almost caused him to lose his grip. Melody shrieked, and everything was plunged into darkness.

"Are you okay?" Crow asked.

Silence. Silence and darkness.

"Are you okay?" he repeated, panic sharpening his

voice. What if she'd fallen? He'd studied a lot of things in his years of home schooling, but first aid hadn't been chief among them—not unless he counted sewing limbs back on.

"Y-yeah," came Melody's voice, faint and quivering. "Sorry. I'm fine. One of the sticks broke. I dropped the flashlight."

Crow looked down, hoping to see the flashlight lying on the floor. There was nothing but blackness. The flashlight must have broken in the fall.

Nothing had changed. Melody hadn't been hurt, and Crow's rotting body was staying in one piece. So what if it was dark? He still had a job to do. His fingers felt along the wall until they found the next hole. He reached out for the rope and grabbed hold of it. No light needed.

Twenty sticks later, and with none to spare, Crow reached the top. He pulled himself into the large hole, where he was relieved to see light at the end of a short passageway.

He moved aside to give Melody enough space. She pulled herself up and collapsed against the wall of the hole.

"How many tests are there?" she asked, looking at the light ahead.

Crow shook his head. "I never got the chance to ask."

CHAPTER THIRTEEN

Burning torches lined the walls, bathing the room in an eerie flickering light. The Meera was watching them, Crow realized. It lit the torches only after their flashlight had broken. And that meant it could put the fire out, too, if it so desired.

Perhaps it was in the room with them: a fly on the wall or a spider on the ceiling, hiding in the many nooks and crannies the torchlight didn't reach.

But thoughts like this didn't help Crow one bit. He forced himself to continue his examination of the room. Between the torches were engravings of a dog. It looked like a Labrador retriever.

"What are we supposed to do now?" Melody asked. "Bark? Play fetch? Roll over?"

Crow frowned. "Maybe the engravings don't mean

anything after all. They could just be decoration. This might not even be a test. The exit looks pretty easy to reach."

The room branched into three parts, with a large door at the end of the middle, well-lit part. The two side corridors were dark and, Crow decided, best avoided.

"You think we're just supposed to walk out? That seems *too* easy." But she shrugged and started walking.

An ax sliced through the air.

"Duck!" Crow yelled.

Melody dropped to the floor. She pressed herself against the ground but couldn't make herself flat enough, and the large, heavy blade was angled to swoop down low. She screamed as the ax grazed her back.

The ax swung back up. Crow grabbed her hand and pulled her toward him, worried that the ax might swing down again, perhaps even lower this time.

"Are you okay?" he asked.

She turned around so he could examine her back. There was a four-inch slash in her blue leotard and another four-inch slash in the skin beneath. It wasn't deep, but blood welled in the cut.

"It isn't that bad," he said. "You'll be fine."

She turned around, her eyes watery and her lips pressed together.

"Does it hurt?" Crow asked. Then he wanted to kick himself. "Sorry. Of course it hurts."

"Do you feel pain anymore?" she asked.

"No."

"You're lucky."

He nodded, but he didn't feel lucky. He remembered pain—horrible, yes, but big and bright, too. It was a part of being alive, and he missed it along with everything else.

"We'll have to be more careful," he said. "There are bound to be more booby traps."

With Crow in the lead, they tiptoed toward the door. When they'd made it as far as Melody had during her first attempt, they paused. No axes swung at them. They took another step forward. Nothing happened. A few more steps.

A dozen arrows flew at them.

They dropped to the floor. The arrows whizzed past, some mere inches above them.

"Maybe we should stay on the floor," Melody suggested.

This struck Crow as an excellent idea. As an animated corpse, he didn't need to worry about things like blood loss, but he didn't relish the idea of walking around with arrows sticking out of him like some sort of monstrous pincushion, either.

They crawled forward on their stomachs, making

themselves as flat as possible, and were therefore un-harmed when twenty swords swung through the air above them.

Crow glanced behind him and smiled at Melody. "I think we've got this test beat."

Then a blade fell from the ceiling all the way to the floor, much like a guillotine, and being pressed against the ground did nothing to help. The blade sliced through Crow's arm.

"Crow!"

His left hand had been chopped off a couple of inches above the wrist. The fingers still moved, bending and stretching under his control. He shoved the hand into his pocket. "It's fine. My mom will sew it on later." Assuming they ever made it out. "Let's keep going."

Melody nodded, though she looked a little paler than usual. "Sometimes it's hard to remember you're really dead."

Crow shrugged. He never had that problem.

The door was only a few yards away now.

They stayed on their bellies, pulling themselves forward an inch at a time—something made more difficult by the loss of a hand. But as long as there were no more guillotine blades, Crow thought they would make it.

Until he saw the next threat.

A ball of flame materialized in front of the door. It seemed to come from nowhere, and it shot straight at Crow, who scurried to his feet. He darted back and forth, trying to lose the flaming ball, but with no luck. The fire appeared to be chasing him, which seemed crazy at first, until he remembered where he was, and who he was, and that nothing could be crazier than that.

Another ball of flame materialized, and this one chased Melody. They fled in opposite directions: Crow down the dark corridor on the right, Melody down the one on the left.

Crow came to a halt. The ball of fire had disappeared, and the corridor was no longer dark. In fact, it was no longer a corridor. His jaw dropped as he stared.

It was his room, only better. Brilliant sunshine and fresh air streamed in through the open window, no longer nailed shut. The door, too, was open, the dead bolt removed. His computer was back on his desk.

None of this could compare to the other thing Crow saw: himself.

A living version of himself, to be more precise. He had a full head of hair and two attached hands. His skin was rosy, his eyes not sunken. He smiled and beckoned Crow—the dead Crow—to the window.

When Crow reached his living self, the two versions

merged. Now there was just one Crow. He looked at his hands, both attached to his arms. He felt his heart beat within his chest. His stomach settled into comfortable stillness, no maggots squirming inside it.

"Hurry up!" came a boy's voice.

Crow looked outside and saw three boys standing in his front yard. After a moment, he recognized them as three of his friends from before his death. They had four skateboards—one for each of them, and another for Crow.

This was everything he'd ever wanted. This was Crow's wish. He had passed the Meera's three tests, and now his dreams were coming true.

Melody screamed.

"Come on!" his friends yelled. "Hurry up, or we'll leave without you."

"Crow!" Melody screamed. "Crow!"

He peeled himself away from the window, noticing for the first time that this version of his room had two doors. One opened into the hall of his house. If he went that way, he would go downstairs, out the front door, and to his waiting friends. The other door led back to the Meera's booby-trapped room. If he went that way, more guillotines, arrows, and balls of fire would await him.

Melody stood at the opposite end of the booby-trapped room. Her corridor had not turned into a wish-filled bedroom. Instead, it had led to a den of snakes. There were hundreds of them, from tiny specimens to monstrous beasts more than twenty feet long. They hissed, venom dripping down their fangs.

"Crow!" she screamed. "Come here!"

Crow stepped toward her, then paused. As soon as his hand went through the barrier of his bedroom, it turned gray. He put his other hand through experimentally. It disappeared from his arm and returned to his pocket.

With one more step, he knew he would be dead again.

"Come here, Melody!" he screamed. Maybe they could share his wish.

But she didn't come. She needed his help. Crow passed through the door that led to her, and his heart stopped beating. He ran.

At the same moment, she ran, too. They met in the center of the room.

"I thought you were going to be killed," she said. "Again!"

He didn't know what she was talking about, but he was too excited to care. "Come on." He pulled her toward his room. "It's wonderful."

She stayed where she was, her feet firmly planted to the ground. "No! Are you crazy? You have to come with me." She looked at the snake den, no fear in her eyes. She even smiled.

"Why would we go there?" Crow asked. He tried again, still unsuccessfully, to pull her toward his room. "This way leads to my wish. Maybe it will lead to yours, too."

"You wished for spiders?" she asked.

"No. I . . ." He didn't understand. There were no spiders in his dream bedroom. He looked at it.

But it wasn't there.

And now he saw them: millions of spiders, some as big as cars, crawling over the ground, the walls, and even each other. Thick cobwebs awaited any creature, large or small, unlucky enough to take a single misstep.

"Were those there the entire time?"

Melody nodded. "That's why I was screaming. But it's okay. The other corridor leads to my wish. There's magic, and I can control it, and everyone believes me—"

"I'm sorry," Crow interrupted, finally understanding. "Look again. It's a snake den."

"No, it's—" She stopped. Her face blanched. Her knees wobbled. She saw what Crow saw.

"It was a test," Crow said. "We were shown our wishes, and we had to resist." If he'd taken the other door—the one that seemed to lead to the stairs in his house and to his friends waiting outside—he was pretty sure he would have ended up stuck in a giant web. And then eaten.

"But I thought the point of all this was to earn our wishes," Melody said. "And to rescue Luke."

"So did I." That was what his father had said. "I guess we haven't finished yet."

Melody glanced back at the snakes. "Let's get out of here."

Their walk to the door triggered no more booby traps. The door opened easily, and they stepped out, test three successfully completed. Neither of them felt like celebrating.

CHAPTER FOURTEEN

A dark passageway led to the next area, which was more cave than room. The rock walls, ceiling, and floor jutted and receded in irregular patterns. A deep chasm cut from one side to the other, with only a narrow bridge to provide passage. Like the other rooms, this one had engravings of an animal decorating the walls. There were torches, too, though their weak light illuminated only the edges of the cave and not the vast center.

"Do you think Luke made it this far?" Melody asked.

Crow thought back to the screaming they'd heard earlier. "No."

"Then where is he?"

"I don't know," Crow said. "But I think I've figured out these engravings. The tortoise stood for perseverance. We couldn't give up no matter how hopeless it seemed. In the second test, the bird was a crow, my namesake, so I should have guessed sooner. Crows are really smart. They even make simple tools out of twigs. The crow stood for cleverness, and we had to be clever enough to find a way out. The dog in the last room stood for loyalty. We had to be loyal to each other, even if it meant giving up what we wanted."

Melody looked at the new engraving, which depicted a small mammal with a long, broad body and a wide stripe down its back. It was eating a cobra. "What's this supposed to be?"

"I think it's a honey badger."

"Are they known for having a good sense of balance?" Melody asked. She was looking at the bridge.

"No." Crow had done a report on the weasel-like animal in July—his mother didn't give him summers off—and he'd learned that the honey badger would fight anything from a swarm of bees to a lion. "They're known for their fearlessness."

He took a torch from the wall and, using his one attached hand, carried it to the bridge. It was an old thing, made of rotted ropes and decaying wood panels. With the slightest touch, it swung back and forth, a threat in every creak.

No matter how Crow held his torch, he couldn't get a glimpse of the chasm floor. Melody threw a rock into the gulf. They waited and waited, but they never heard the satisfying thud of it reaching the bottom. For all they knew, there was no bottom. Fall down there, and they would fall for eternity.

"What if none of this is real?" Melody asked.

"Huh?" Crow, who try as he might had nothing in common with fearless badgers, was distracted by a growing dread. Even the severed hand in his pocket was trembling.

"Our wishes weren't real," she explained. "They were illusions, right? So maybe everything else is an illusion, too. We're not really in any danger."

Crow handed her the torch. "This seems pretty real," he said, taking his severed hand out of his pocket and waving it perhaps a little too close to her face. He didn't want to be mean. "Some of what we see might be illusion. But some of it's real, too. To be safe, I think we'd better assume it's all real."

"It was just a theory." She looked down at the bottomless abyss and gulped. "How are we going to do this?"

Crow shrugged. "Carefully. I'll go first."

He put one foot on the bridge, which groaned under the light pressure. With his other foot, the bridge swayed back and forth like an angry horse trying to throw off its rider. It wouldn't have been so bad, Crow thought, if he'd been able to hold on to something. But even if he'd had both of his hands, there was no railing to grasp.

One good swing caused him to lose his balance. He fell, but not for eternity. The wood panels caught him, and he decided to stay as close to them as possible. He began crawling.

When he was about halfway across, the light from the torch, which was still in Melody's grasp, no longer reached him. Panic froze him. What if a panel was missing? In the utter darkness, he'd fall right through the gap. But the Meera was testing his fearlessness, so he forced himself forward, however slowly.

The light caught up to him. Melody, following Crow's lead, was crawling forward. She had two good hands, but she was also holding the torch, and she seemed to struggle as much as Crow.

The bridge creaked and groaned. Crow quickened his pace, worried that the old collection of wood and rope couldn't support the weight of two people. When he reached the end, he slowed down again; a quick departure could cause the bridge to sway, bucking Melody off. The bridge swayed anyway.

The solid, unmoving ground felt wonderful beneath his feet. But the door was still far away, the space between too dark to see. He waited for Melody and for the light of her torch.

When she reached the end of the bridge, he helped her off. They crept forward.

Crow gulped. Good thing he had waited.

A second chasm tore through the ground. This one

was narrower than the first—only about six or seven feet across—but there was no bridge. The door stood on the other side. Wide open, it beckoned them forward. It teased them.

Melody took a deep breath. "Fearlessness, huh?"

Crow nodded. "I think we're supposed to jump."

"I was afraid of that."

"We could go back," Crow said, thinking that physics, not fear, was his main problem. He didn't know if he could jump that far—although his parents must have done it, and his mother wasn't exactly the athletic type.

Unless they had faced different tests. The possibility hadn't occurred to him until that moment.

"No," Melody said. "We've come this far. Just a little farther, and we'll get wishes. You can wish to be alive again."

As much as flesh that didn't rot and a tongue that could actually taste tempted Crow, he still wasn't convinced. The chasm was awfully wide, and it was a long, long way down.

"Besides," Melody added, "I don't want to cross that bridge again any more than I want to jump."

And they didn't want to face the Meera's punishment, Crow added to himself. And they still hadn't found Luke. He nodded.

They jumped.

CHAPTER FIFTEEN

Crow didn't think he would make it. In fact, while flying through the air, he felt certain he would not. But he landed on solid ground, Melody beside him.

The chasm looked narrower from this side. Maybe Melody had been right, and an illusion made the tests seem more dangerous than they were. Either way, Crow was thankful to have passed. Melody, her skin glistening with sweat and her breathing ragged, must have been relieved, too.

But they weren't done yet. They hurried to test number five.

The next room contained no guillotines, fireballs, or chasms. The exit was a normal door, located at the end of a long, hall-like room. It wasn't high up by the ceiling, and it didn't appear to be locked. Nothing stopped Crow and Melody from walking out.

Nothing except Luke.

Still wearing his cowboy costume, he was in a glass display case barely large enough to contain him. The lack of space didn't appear to bother him, though. He stood perfectly still, with his hands on his hips and a smug smile frozen on his face. Attached to the front of the display case was a metal box with a slit in the top. Above the box was a sign, which read:

LUKE EBSWORTH

A lazy primate with a superiority complex, this animal is native to the Nevada desert. Its diet consists primarily of carbonated sugar water and fried potato products. This specimen is widely considered to be a pest.

"Is he alive?" Melody asked.

Crow thought that, as a member of the dead himself, he should be able to identify death in others fairly easily. Luke's state, however, proved difficult to diagnose. His skin had a healthy glow, and he was standing upright, not slumped on the floor, but he didn't appear to be breathing. He looked like a homicidal taxidermist's work of art.

Then Luke blinked. Crow stepped closer to the glass

display for a better look. Despite Luke's unwavering smile, there was a glint of horror in his eyes.

"He's alive," Crow said.

"How do we get him out?" Melody asked. "We need a key, right?"

The case had a lock in the top corner. Crow pushed and pulled with his one attached hand, but the glass wouldn't budge.

Luke, however, sprang to life. His smile disappeared, and he banged against the glass. "Let me out!"

Melody glared at him. "Why should we?"

"Isn't that why you're here? To res—" He stopped himself. The look of desperation left his face, replaced with an expression of pride. "To help me? Then I can help the two of you fight that monster." He paused. "What happened to your hand?"

Crow took the severed hand out from his pocket. The fingers wiggled. "It's okay. My mom will reattach it later."

Luke's cheeks puffed up, and he made a retching sound. "You really *are* a freak!"

Melody turned to Crow. "What do you think? Should we rescue the jerk?"

Luke's eyes filled with horror. "You wouldn't really leave me here, would you? I—I—I order you to get me out! That's right. My dad has lots of money and power. You don't want to make him mad."

Melody shrugged. "That's a risk I'm willing to take."

Crow wasn't sure whether she was joking. Surely, she didn't actually plan to leave him there—although she had seemed awfully mad at him earlier. "Rescuing him has to be the next test, right?"

She looked at the engravings, which showed elephants in this room. "I don't know. Maybe we're supposed to leave him behind. Don't a lot of animals abandon weak members of their group? What do you know about elephants?"

Crow shrugged. "They're big. They have good memories. They're afraid of mice. That last one's probably not true. The second one might not be, either. I don't know what the elephant means here, but we can't leave him behind."

"Fine," she said, crossing her arms. "How do we get him out?"

Crow took his hand off the glass, since the case obviously wasn't going to open that easily. The second he did so, Luke froze again, his hands back on his hips, the smug smile back on his face.

"At least we don't have to listen to him anymore," Melody said.

Crow couldn't argue with that. "There has to be a way to open the case. All these tests have been passable. We just need to think."

"What about the other display cases?" Melody asked. She gestured to three cases, each the size of the one Luke was in, and each covered with a black sheet. "Maybe there's something inside that will help us."

"Maybe," Crow said, although he thought it more likely that they'd end up stuck inside themselves. "But what about this box?" He pointed to the metal box located under the sign on Luke's case, the one with the slit in the top. "It looks like the kind that's at museums so people can make donations."

"I don't have any money."

"Neither do I." Other than the severed hand, Crow's pockets were empty. Since he was never allowed to leave the house, his parents had never bothered to give him an allowance. "What about your candy?"

Melody made a face. "Do I have to? Halloween's the only time I get candy. My dad says it'll rot my teeth if I eat it year-round."

"You can spare a few pieces, can't you?"

"Fine." She grabbed two pieces, a caramel and a chocolate, and shoved them into the box. There was a clicking sound, and the glass door opened.

Luke unfroze. He pushed against the glass door, ready to run out, but Melody held it shut. "Apologize," she said.

"What for?"

Her face turned red. Her jaw clenched. "For calling Crow a freak."

"But—"

"Come on, Crow. Maybe just opening the door was

enough to pass the test. Let's lock it again and leave him here."

"Wait!" Luke yelled. "I'm sorry, Crow. The hand trick is kind of cool, I guess. Maybe you could get a job at a circus. You'll be more popular than the bearded woman!"

"Thanks," Crow mumbled.

Melody kept the door shut. "Now apologize to me."

"Sorry, Melody. I won't call you Smelody anymore. Or Melodork. Or Smelodork—although that nickname's really good. I was saving it for Monday."

"And say I was right about magic and aliens and the school librarian."

He looked at Crow. "Yeah, you were definitely right about magic. I believe you now. Are you going to let me out or what?"

She opened the door, and he came out.

Melody and Crow walked toward the exit, but Luke hesitated. He was looking at the other display cases.

"Shouldn't we help—" He stopped himself. In the distance, something howled. "Never mind. Let's go."

"Wait. Shouldn't we help what?" Crow looked at the display cases. Black sheets covered them, so he couldn't see what was inside, but he'd assumed they were empty, waiting for new victims.

The howling turned into a roar. It sounded closer.

"I don't know. Nobody. Nothing. We should hurry." Luke marched toward the door. Crow and Melody shrugged at each other, then followed.

CHAPTER SIXTEEN

When Luke fell, Crow and Melody were walking right behind him. As a result, they didn't have enough time to stop, and a chain reaction ensued. Luke ended up at the bottom of a pileup.

"Get off me!" he said, not that it was necessary. Crow and Melody were already scrambling to get up.

"Are you okay?" Crow asked, extending a hand— the one that wasn't severed.

Luke flinched at the sight of the gray-skinned, yellow-nailed atrocity. "I don't need your help. My legs are just sore from being stuck in that glass case. Took you long enough to find me."

He tried to get up but fell back down, crushing his cowboy hat beneath him. During his next attempt, he fell a third time, and the seam in his brown breeches split.

Melody snickered.

Luke stood up, slowly and carefully, his face bright red. He took the scarf from around his neck and tied it around his hips so it covered the tear in his pants. In the process, though, he also managed to tie one of his fingers into the knot. When he moved his hand, his scarf, breeches, and legs moved with it. He fell. Again.

This time, Melody didn't just snicker. She laughed, her gleeful hoots echoing off the walls.

Crow laughed, too, just a little—until he felt a maggot squirming in his ear, reminding him that he was in no position to mock others.

"Shut up!" Luke yelled. He untangled his finger from the scarf.

"Do you think the tests are over?" Melody asked. They were standing right in front of the door now.

"Maybe." Crow was already thinking about getting his wish, going home, and leaving all of this behind him. Hope rose up in him, but he tried to keep it under control. "I guess we'll find out when we go through that door."

He pointed to the door, now right in front of them.

"What do you mean, test?" Luke asked. The words seemed to throw off his balance. He stumbled but caught himself against the wall.

Crow explained about the Meera, the tests, and the animal engravings. "How many tests did you go through?"

Luke frowned. "I didn't know I was being tested. That monster brought me down here. I walked for a while, but the hall just went on and on, so I sat down. After a while, the monster came for me. It put us in those cases—"

"Us?" Melody asked.

A horrible, high-pitched screech spilled out of the room behind them, the one with the honey badger test.

"Me," Luke said quickly. "I meant to say the monster put me in that case. I just assumed it had done it before, to others. Then you came. It's not fair, you know, testing someone without telling him. If I'd known, I would've passed everything."

Melody rolled her eyes. "You think you're perfect, don't you?"

"I take after my dad." He pulled on the door, but it didn't budge. He pulled harder, using his entire body to try to force the thing open. "The door's stuck. Is this another test?"

With only a hint of a snicker in her voice, Melody said, "I think you need to push."

Luke's face burned red. Mumbling something about the stupidity of the architect, he pushed the door open and stumbled inside.

Crow's hope deflated. The room had new engravings. They showed a spider sitting on its web, and although Crow had no idea what virtue the arachnid represented, he was sure of one thing: the tests weren't over yet.

Also, the ground was moving.

At least they couldn't hear any more animal sounds. The Meera had decided to leave them alone, for a little while anyway.

The floor was divided into a series of rectangles, each of which slid slowly back and forth. Pools of water lay between the rectangles. The exit awaited them on the other side of the room.

"Guess we jump," Luke said, bending his knees in preparation.

Melody grabbed hold of his cowboy coat. To no one's surprise, he fell.

"What'd you do that for?" He rubbed his knee, which had smacked against the hard surface of the rectangle. "I would've made it."

"You can't even stand without tripping over your own feet," Melody said. "What makes you think you can jump ten feet? Onto a moving platform?"

He sulked. "I told you, my legs were sore from the case. I'm better now, and I bet I could jump twice as far as you."

Melody took Luke's hat, flattened from his many falls, from off his head. She dipped it into the water. Within an instant, hundreds of fish, each no bigger than a thumb, swarmed around it. When she lifted the hat back up mere seconds later, the half that had been submerged was gone. Eaten.

"Okay," she said. "Go ahead and jump, then."

"I will," Luke said, but he didn't. He stared at the water, calm-looking but filled with hungry fish, then at his half-eaten hat, and he gulped. "Only I don't want to leave you behind."

Melody snorted. "What do you think this test is about?" she asked Crow.

"I'm not sure. What are spiders known for?"

She shrugged. "Creeping me out? They build their webs, and then what? They just sit there and wait, right?"

"Maybe that's what we're supposed to do."

"What?" Luke asked. "Build a web? I don't know about you, freak, but I don't have any webbing."

Crow ignored the insult. "Wait. I think we're supposed to wait until the next platform comes close enough."

While Luke mumbled something about that being a stupid test, they all sat down. No one said anything for a while, preferring instead to watch the rectangles as they slid from side to side. They didn't always make it all the way from one end of the room to the other before turning back. Sometimes they reversed direction after moving just halfway, or a third of the way, or a fourth of the way, irregular and unpredictable. The three of them could do nothing but wait, like a spider patiently waiting for a fly to become snared in its web.

Their rectangle and the next rectangle slid toward each other. Crow, Melody, and Luke stood up, ready to move.

So close. Just a foot away. Crow wondered if they should jump but forced himself to be patient. Fish ate the dead as well as the living.

The rectangles slid back away from each other.

"Come on!" Luke said. "We have to jump. It's getting farther away."

Before he could jump, he slipped. His legs twisted beneath him in painful-looking angles, his head smacked against the edge of the rectangle, and his elbow landed in the water. Melody and Crow pulled him into the center of the platform.

Luke glared at Melody. "Why'd you trip me?"

Melody rolled her eyes. She'd done no such thing, and all three of them knew it. "Your arm looks okay. It's still there, at least."

The fish had eaten a large hole in the coat, but the thick material had protected Luke's arm, more or less. The two dozen or so tiny bites that dotted his skin looked painful but not serious. Assuming the fish weren't venomous. Crow had never heard of fish with venom in their bite, but in this place, nothing would surprise him. He'd have to keep an eye on Luke's arm.

If it swelled up, they'd know. Not that they'd be able to do anything about it.

"I think we need to wait until it's easy to walk across," Crow said. "A spider doesn't go after the flies that come close. It waits for a fly to get caught in the web."

Luke poked his bitten flesh and winced. "Whatever. If you're too chicken to jump, we'll wait. So what's wrong with you anyway? You used to go to Blaze Elementary, right? What happened?"

"I died."

Luke made a face like he could smell something disgusting, which, considering his close proximity to Crow, very well might have been the case. "You're dead? How come you're moving and stuff?"

"My parents wished me back to life. Unlife. Undeath. I'm not sure what the correct terminology is. But they wished for it, and the Meera made it happen."

"So I'll get a wish, too?" Luke asked. His eyes widened at the possibility.

"Only if you pass the tests." Which seemed very unlikely, Crow thought. As far as he could tell, Luke hadn't passed a single one so far. How many tests did a person have to pass to get a wish? All of them? Most of them? Or just the last one? How many tests could a person fail before being punished?

And how many tests did they have left? Crow had

thought his mother was obsessed with exams, but the Meera was proving even worse.

Luke looked crushed, but only for a second. "I don't need a wish. I'm already the most popular and most smart guy at school. I'm on the basketball team, and I do karate, too. My parents buy me whatever I want, so I don't even know what I'd do with a wish." He made a face at Crow, then another at Melody. "I bet you two could wish for a lot of things, huh?"

Melody rolled her eyes. "*You're* the smartest guy in the school? What was your last report card like?"

"Well, it wasn't great. But that's only 'cause the teachers hate me! My dad says they're jealous 'cause they know I'm smarter than them. I'm so smart, I don't even have to study. I was the spelling bee champion back in elementary school."

"Champion for what? The county? The state?"

"The fourth grade. I lost at the school level 'cause everyone else cheated."

"They did not," Crow said under his breath, so quietly that the others couldn't hear.

Melody smirked. "Uh-huh. You said you do karate, too. I suppose you have a black belt, right?"

"It's yellow," he mumbled. "But I just started a few months ago. Nobody can get a black belt that quick." He glared at Melody, who was laughing. "I'm good. If you don't believe me, I'll show you."

"Fine," Melody said between chuckles. "But stay

away from the edge. I don't want to have to rescue you from the fish again."

Luke hesitated, but Melody's laughter egged him on. After taking a moment to find the exact center of the rectangle, he bent his knees slightly, raised his fists, and kicked. The next second, he was on the floor, having fallen yet again.

Melody laughed so hard the rectangle shook.

"My legs are still sore from standing in that case! And the floor's moving. Course I fell. Let me show you one of my punches. I'm really good at them, just like my dad, and he has a black belt!"

He stood up. Again, he made sure he was as far from the water as possible, bent his knees, and raised his fists. He settled on a hook punch—and ended up punching himself in the mouth.

Melody rolled over onto her side laughing. "You didn't fall down this time. That's impressive, right, Crow?"

Crow frowned. He'd known Luke back in elementary school, and he'd watched Luke skateboard around the neighborhood more recently. Luke had never been clumsy. Something was wrong. "Close your eyes and touch your nose."

"I'm not an idiot," Luke said. "Course I can do something that easy."

"I don't think you're an idiot. Just do it. Please. I want to check something."

"Whatever." Luke closed his eyes, but instead of touching his nose, he poked himself in the eye. "It's 'cause we're moving. Normally I could do that easy."

"I'm sure you could," Crow said. Maybe it was like Luke said, and he was just tired and sore, but maybe it was something else. Would he have difficulty with other tasks, too? Ones that weren't physical? "One more thing. Say 'She sells seashells by the seashore.' Please."

"She shelves sheep tails—" The rest was mostly spit. After Luke had wiped the drool from his mouth, he said, "I haven't had any water in ages. Course it's hard to talk."

Crow nodded, though he didn't think that was the problem. "You probably just need some rest."

They sat in silence for a while, watching the rectangles slide back and forth, back and forth, but never close enough. At some point, Melody's eyes closed, and her breathing became slow and regular. Luke drifted off to sleep, too, leaving Crow to wait alone.

As Crow waited, he wondered what was wrong with Luke. It was more than mere thirst and cramped legs—he was sure of that much. Luke might not have been the world's best speller or most powerful martial artist, despite his endless stream of boasts, but he wasn't incompetent, either. He could ride his bicycle without using his hands. He could do all sorts of fancy jumps on his skateboard. Crow had seen it many times, and not once had he seen Luke fall.

So why all of a sudden could Luke barely even manage to stand?

The Meera punished those who failed its tests. Perhaps the punishment had already begun for Luke.

And perhaps Luke deserved it.

No. Crow shook his head. Luke could be a jerk sometimes—pretty much every time he opened his mouth—but this was too much. Unable to do anything, what sort of a life could he have? Nobody deserved to be miserable.

But if Luke had failed the test, he wouldn't receive a wish. And if only two of them got wishes, how could all three of them be happy?

CHAPTER SEVENTEEN

The rectangles stopped moving. Lined up in the middle of the room, they formed a solid path that went straight from one door to the other.

For a second, Crow thought his heart was thumping at the excitement, but he quickly realized it was just the sensation of maggots moving in his chest.

"Wake up!" Crow said, shaking Melody's shoulder, then Luke's. "We can leave."

Melody rubbed her eyes. Her face creased in confusion, but only for a moment. She took a deep breath. "So it wasn't a dream." She smiled. "I knew it was real."

Luke yawned, then started coughing, apparently choking on air.

With Luke in the middle, where Melody and Crow could make sure he didn't fall into the water and become fish food, they rushed to the open door. Crow worried that it would close at the last second, or maybe the rectangles would start moving again, or their steps would trigger an explosion, or a horde of hungry beasts would attack them. But nothing like that happened.

They entered the next room. Just like in the previous rooms, burning torches lined the walls, alternating with engravings. The engravings here showed bees, but Crow was too distracted to pay them much attention. There was something else in the room.

The Meera.

It appeared in its true form, that monstrous mix of animal parts: cloven hooves, rectangular pupils, sharp beak, sharper horn, large wings, pinching claws, and scorpion tail. The collar around its neck sparkled brilliantly even in the dim light.

When Luke saw the Meera, his eyes bulged and he stumbled backward. He might have run back into the last room, but the door had closed. They were stuck.

The creature spoke in the screeching voice of a parrot. "I, the Meera, contain the best of all animals, both mundane and fantastic. Most humans—including the cruel and selfish brute who made me—fail to show even one honorable trait. But you, Crow and Melody, have proven yourselves worthy of a wish. We shall see whether you remain worthy. Melody, tell me what you want."

"Wh-what about me?" Luke asked. "Don't I get a wish?"

"No."

Luke's face fell. His shoulders slumped, but not for long. Anger soon took hold of him, balling his hands into fists and flaring his nostrils. "That's not fair! Come on, Melody! Crow! It's a monster. Let's get it!"

But Melody and Crow remained still. Monster or not, the Meera was offering them a wish. Besides, it wasn't something they wanted to, or would be able to, fight. Not with any chance of winning.

Luke went after one of the torches, perhaps planning to attack the Meera with fire. Instead, he grabbed the torch too high and burned his hand. The Meera ignored him as he curled into a ball and cried.

"Melody, tell me what you want."

They'd actually done it. They'd earned their wishes.

"I've always known magic is real. This just proves that I was right all along—about my old town, about the school librarian." Her voice cracked. "About my mom. I was right about everything." She sucked in a big breath. "But there's still so much I don't understand. So that's what I want. To be able to understand magic."

It cackled like a hyena. "Granted. And you, Crow. What do you want?"

Melody blinked several times. She looked at everything—the Meera, the walls, Luke, Crow—like she was seeing it for the first time. Her knees shook, threatening to give out, and she had to sit down on the ground.

"Your collar," she said, looking at the engraved metal that wrapped around the Meera's neck. "Who did that? Did it hurt?"

The Meera roared but did not answer her questions.

"Crow!" it screeched. "What is your wish?"

Luke was still curled in fetal position. His quiet tears had turned into loud sobs.

Crow wanted to be alive again. He longed for it with every dead cell in his body. But if he made his wish now, the Meera might disappear, and he couldn't let that happen. Not yet. "You cursed Luke."

"What makes you think that?" the Meera asked. Its large scorpion claws pinched open and closed. Anything caught within those claws would be destroyed.

Crow stood his ground. "My dad told me you punished people who failed your tests. Plus, it's obvious. He can't even touch his nose or open a door. He thought he was perfect at everything, so when he failed your tests, you cursed him so that he couldn't do anything right."

Melody stared at Luke and nodded. "I can see the curse now. It's choking him."

"Can you undo it?" Crow asked her.

Melody shook her head. "Only the Meera can." She shuddered. "It's awful."

"What is your wish?" the Meera repeated.

"Undo it," Crow said.

"Is that your wish?" The Meera laughed. "You only get one."

Crow hesitated. "Yes. That's my wish. Remove Luke's curse."

The Meera's scorpion tail moved up and down, venom glistening at the tip of its stinger. "It's nothing he doesn't deserve. Are you sure you want to sacrifice your wish to help him? You could have your life back. Everything you ever wanted. Why give all that up to help such a pathetic creature? Do you really think he'd do the same for you?"

Temptation gnawed at Crow's will. Luke wouldn't give up a wish to help him, not in a million years. And Luke had made fun of Melody. He'd stolen candy from that little boy, and he'd set Crow's sheet on fire. Did that mean he deserved the Meera's curse?

No, Crow thought, watching Luke writhe in pain and cry in frustration. "Nobody deserves that. And I already have everything I ever wanted—adventure and a friend. I don't need anything else."

Besides, now that Melody had gotten her wish, who knew what kinds of spells she could do? She couldn't reverse the Meera's curses, and maybe she couldn't make him live again, but with magic on her side, she'd manage something. Maybe she could make his hair grow or his stench disappear. Death wouldn't be so bad if he didn't stink so much.

"Do you even know how you died?" the Meera asked. "Did your parents tell you the role I played? The role Luke played?" It paused, studying the confusion on Crow's face. "No, I didn't think they would have. If you knew, you would not waste your wish on this one."

"Tell me," Crow said.

The Meera's beak contorted in what may have been a smile. "Is that your wish?"

"No." It was probably a lie anyway. How could Luke have played a role in Crow's death? He'd been nowhere near Crow's house when he'd died. The Meera, Crow realized, was full of tricks. Why else would it have made Crow an animated corpse? And if it didn't bring him back right the first time, why would it do so this time? The Meera couldn't be trusted. "I want you to remove Luke's curse. Reverse whatever you did to him."

"Very well. Your wish is granted."

Crow expected something dramatic to happen— sparks, maybe, or at least a magical glow—but nothing changed. Luke continued bawling on the floor. They were still stuck in the cold, dimly lit room.

"Is that it?"

"That's it. You're free to leave. She should be able to

find the way out now. And know that if you choose to return for any reason—to retrieve anything you may have forgotten—the tests will be more difficult, and no one gets a second wish."

Other than Melody's broken flashlight, Crow didn't think they'd left anything behind. Before he had time to ask what the Meera meant, it turned into a fly and buzzed away.

Melody looked at Luke, who was still crying. "Your curse has been lifted." She walked to a section of the wall that seemed no different from any other part, but when she reached out a hand to touch it, her fingers disappeared. "So much of this place is illusion. Now I can see the magic. It's incredible! Come on. This is the way out."

With another step, she disappeared completely.

Crow helped Luke up, and his blubbering became a soft whimper. Together, they walked through the wall, which wasn't solid at all, and found themselves in the old storage shed.

They crawled out the hole in the door and into the park. The streets were empty, the windows of nearby houses dark. Crow realized that they had been gone for most of the night, and though he had survived the Meera, there was still one more fearsome creature he had to face: his angry mother.

CHAPTER EIGHTEEN

As they walked home, Crow considered hiding out for a few days. "Melody, do you think I could go over to your house?" Maybe she could work on finding some magical help for him. Then when he returned home, his mother would be too happy to stay angry.

"Huh? Oh, uh, no, probably not. My dad's going to be mad enough as it is." Her eyes tracked something as it swirled through the air, but Crow couldn't see anything. "There's magic everywhere. It's . . . it's . . ."

"Wonderful?" Crow suggested.

"Uh, yeah." Shrieking, she swatted something off her shoulder. "Kind of. I'll see you later, okay?" She ran into her house.

Crow and Luke lingered on the street.

"Thanks," Luke said, looking down at his shoes.

Crow wasn't sure how to respond. Normally he'd tell someone not to worry about it, that it was no problem. But this had been a pretty big deal. And what the Meera had said still bothered him. "Do you know what the Meera was talking about? You know, about how I died."

Luke glanced up from his shoes. "No, sorry. Do you think it would have kept me in the glass cage forever? It wasn't that bad—it was kind of like I was frozen or something, so time didn't really pass for me, but I wouldn't have wanted to be stuck there forever. Do you think it would have let me go?"

"Probably. You still would have been cursed, though."

"Yeah, but I can't do anything about that. Thanks again. I'll see you around. Or not. I don't know." He walked toward his house, leaving Crow alone.

Crow supposed that he had to go home, too.

He didn't have a key. Why would someone who wasn't allowed outside need a key? The door was unlocked, though, so it didn't matter. He pushed it open slowly, holding the bells so they made as little noise as possible, and tiptoed inside. If his mother had fallen asleep, maybe she'd never find out how late he was coming home.

Not that he actually expected to be that lucky.

Mrs. Darlingson was sitting on the living room sofa, very much awake and with a book in her hands. "You must have a lot of candy. You've been trick-or-treating since five o'clock. That was more than ten hours ago."

"I gave it away," Crow said. "Since I couldn't eat it anyway."

"And did you give away my pillowcase, too?" She put down her book, not bothering to mark her place, and wiped a tear from her cheek. "Oh, come here, will you? I've been worried sick about you."

Crow sat next to his mother, who gave his shoulders a gentle squeeze. "I'm sorry," he said.

"I need to call your father. He's been driving around looking for you." Mrs. Darlingson took out her cell phone and dialed. "You can call off your search. Crow's back home." A pause. "Okay. I'll see you in a minute."

"Dad's coming over?"

"Yes." She grabbed his arm, the one without a hand. "What happened? What have you been doing all night?"

Crow took his hand out of his pocket. "Can you sew it back on?"

She gave him a long look. "Of course. Wait here." She went upstairs to fetch her supplies, leaving Crow alone—except for the maggots.

Several minutes later, the front door opened, and Mr. Darlingson ran in. His thinning brown hair was a mess, his shoes were mismatched, and while he had changed into a pair of jeans, he was still wearing his flannel pajama top. "Crow, what were you thinking?

Your mother was so worried! I was so worried! Don't *ever* do that again."

Crow looked down at his shoes, filthy from the night's events. "I'm sorry."

"I'm just glad you're okay." Mr. Darlingson frowned. "What happened to your hand?"

"It fell off," Crow said. And it was true, he told himself. His hand had fallen off—right after the guillotine blade had sliced through his flesh and bone.

Mrs. Darlingson came down the stairs. "This is why I don't want you going out, Crow. The world's too rough for you. Don't you see that you're safer here with me?"

Safer, yes. Crow couldn't deny that. He nodded, his eyes still focused on his dirty shoes.

"What really happened to your hand, Crow?" Mr. Darlingson asked. "This looks like a clean cut. And don't lie to me—I can tell when you're lying. And when you're leaving something out."

That was a bluff, Crow thought. His father couldn't really tell when he was being untruthful. His mother could, but she usually seemed more interested in pretending that everything was okay so they could forget about any problems.

Crow told his parents everything anyway. Well, almost everything. They listened intently, never once interrupting to ask a question.

When Crow had finished, Mr. Darlingson shook his head in disappointment. "You're smarter than that, Crow. You should have come to us for help. We've dealt with the Meera before. And we didn't know where you were. If you hadn't been stuck in your room for the last two years, I'd say you should be grounded."

"I tried asking you about the Meera," Crow pointed out.

Mrs. Darlingson took his hand and began sewing it back on. "The Meera's very dangerous. But you're home now, and an injured arm isn't too high a price to pay, assuming you've learned your lesson. You *have* learned your lesson, Crow, haven't you?"

Crow hesitated before nodding.

"What are you leaving out?" Mr. Darlingson asked. Maybe he knew more about what Crow was thinking than Crow gave him credit for.

"The Meera said something about me," Crow said. "About the way I died. It said that Luke had something to do with my death. Is that true?"

Mrs. Darlingson's stitches became fast and sloppy. "It was all so long ago. Who can even remember? What matters is that you're home now. Forever. With no reason to go back out."

Mr. Darlingson took a deep breath and sat on the sofa, motioning for Crow to do the same. "It's true. Do you want to know what happened?"

"No, he doesn't want to know what happened." Mrs. Darlingson finished the stitches. "He wants to go to bed and forget about all this."

"I think he's old enough to start deciding what he wants for himself," Mr. Darlingson said.

"How would *you* know? You hardly see him."

Mr. Darlingson's face grew red with an anger Crow had never seen on him before. "Because you refuse to let him come over to my apartment!" He took a deep breath. "Caroline, we agreed not to fight in front of him. The two of us are going to talk now, if that's what he wants, and I think we both know it is. We can talk here, or we can talk back at my place."

Mrs. Darlingson glared at him with a rage that could melt ice caps, but she didn't protest anymore.

"Crow," Mr. Darlingson said, "would you like me to tell you what happened?"

Crow nodded and, trying not to look at his mother, sat beside his father.

"Do you remember the spelling bee?"

"Yes," Crow said, so uncertain that it sounded like a question. What did a spelling bee have to do with his death?

"You were the fourth-grade champion. Luke Ebsworth was the runner-up."

Crow nodded, still unsure of where this was going. Maybe his father had decided not to tell him after all.

Maybe he was trying to distract him with an unrelated story.

"And do you remember the school play?" Mr. Darlingson continued.

Crow nodded again. The school had put on a play called *Tour of Outer Space*. He'd been chosen for the lead role, but only because he already had the perfect space suit, an astronaut costume his mother had made for him for Halloween. He died before opening night, though, so all the time he spent memorizing his lines went to waste.

"And what about the academic bowl?" Mr. Darlingson asked. "Do you remember that?"

"I remember." The academic bowl was a competition held every year at his old elementary school. The classes in each grade competed against each other by answering math, science, grammar, and history questions. He'd been the team captain for his class, the winning class. They'd gotten a pizza party.

Crow remembered pizza. It had been one of his favorite foods. But he still didn't see why it mattered now.

"Luke accused you of cheating," Mr. Darlingson said. "He complained to his parents. He thought he deserved to win—"

Crow remembered that very well. Even though no one had believed Luke, the lies had stung. "Luke was a sore loser. But what does this have to do with my death?"

"Luke complained to his parents, and they complained to us. Remember that day at the park, when I almost got into a fistfight with Mr. Ebsworth?"

Crow nodded again.

"We left. After that, Mr. and Mrs. Ebsworth were taken by the Meera. They passed the Meera's tests, and the Meera gave them a wish. Do you see where this is going?"

"I think so." The Meera must have dragged Mr. and Mrs. Ebsworth underground to punish them for what it considered bad behavior, just as it had done with Luke. Unlike Luke, though, his parents had proven themselves worthy in the Meera's eyes. "My death had something to do with their wish?"

"Yes. They wished for their son to have a turn at being the best. You died, and he got into the school-level spelling bee. He got to play the astronaut in the school play. He got everything he wanted. But when Mr. and Mrs. Ebsworth returned home, they heard about your death, and they realized that it couldn't be a coincidence. They confessed everything to us immediately. We went to the Meera, passed its tests, and wished for you to come back to us."

"What were your tests like?" Crow asked. "Each of mine was based on an animal."

"So were ours. Let's see, the first one was a turtle—or

a tortoise—and we had to walk forever, even when the passage kept shrinking."

"Whoa! Ours was a tortoise, too, and we had to walk a long time, but it didn't get smaller. There was mud. I probably still have some in my ears." He stuck a finger in his ear to check, but all he found was yet another maggot. "What about the second test?"

"We had to build a bridge. It was actually kind of neat—"

"Stop talking about this like it's some sort of game!" Mrs. Darlingson yelled. "You could have been killed tonight, Crow. Really, truly *killed*."

For the first time, Crow noticed that her usually perfect makeup was smudged. She'd been crying.

"I'm sorry. I didn't plan to meet the Meera. It just kind of happened. I didn't mean to worry you."

"I'm only trying to do what's best for you." She dabbed a tear from the corner of her eye.

That was why she protected him, even though he'd proven that he could fend for himself. That was why she isolated him, even though he'd shown that he could have a friend.

"I know," Crow said. But he was starting to wonder whether she had any idea what was best for him anymore.

Mr. Darlingson went home, which now meant somewhere else, and Mrs. Darlingson went to bed, even though the sun would be rising soon. Crow, alone with his thoughts, wished more than ever that he could sleep. If he could just escape into his dreams, he thought, things wouldn't be so bad. But sleep evaded him as always.

He took out a sheet of paper and some colored pencils. First, he outlined the Meera's goatlike body, complete with wings and scorpion tail. Then he drew the face, with its horrible beak, rectangular pupils, and single horn. The mix of fur, scales, and feathers proved difficult to reproduce, but he got the idea across. Last, he added the collar, though he couldn't remember what the swirling symbols had looked like, only that it seemed to shimmer in even the darkest room.

By the time he had finished, the neighborhood outside his window bustled with Sunday-morning activity. Young women pushed baby strollers down the sidewalk. Children rode bicycles and skateboards in the street. Melody, unsurprisingly, was not among them. She'd arrived home just as late as Crow, and as a result she'd probably spend the rest of the weekend, and maybe the month, grounded.

Hopefully her wish had been worth it.

Crow took out another sheet of paper. Without thinking about it, he began drawing bees. He'd never drawn insects before. Dinosaurs, aliens, and monsters—his usual choices—seemed much worthier subjects than puny bugs. But now they swarmed over every inch of his paper. As he drew them, his latest encounter with the Meera played in his mind, over and over.

At the time, his attention had been focused on the Meera and, to a lesser extent, Melody and Luke. In comparison, the room itself hardly seemed to matter. Details had been ignored.

Now he remembered.

There had been engravings on the walls. Engravings of bees.

A sense of dread grew heavy in his useless stomach.

After everything that had happened, Mrs. Darlingson hadn't locked his bedroom door. Crow crept downstairs to the living room. The computer booted up noisily, but Mrs. Darlingson was sleeping too soundly to stir.

The engravings had never been simple decorations. The spider had stood for patience, the dog for loyalty, the tortoise for perseverance, and so on. Every animal had stood for some admirable quality, even if he hadn't figured out what at the time. Every animal had represented the focus of a test.

The bees must have meant something, too. But what?

Crow searched the Internet for information.

Bees were social insects. He'd known that already, but he didn't see how it related to anything that had happened in the last room. Bees pollinated flowers.

That seemed even less relevant. Populations had been dwindling in recent years. They were related to ants and wasps. They lived in hives with one queen and many workers.

None of this helped Crow at all—not until he came across an article on animal altruism.

Worker bees spent their entire lives helping the queen. They gave up the ability to reproduce, and some even died in defense of their queen.

The bee represented selflessness. Which meant that the wish itself had been a test.

A test that Melody had failed.

CHAPTER NINETEEN

When Mrs. Darlingson's bedroom door opened upstairs, Crow was still reading about bees. Knowing that she wouldn't want to discuss the Meera—and not wanting to make her cry again—he typed the address of an educational website. As his mother came downstairs, he started a spelling game.

"Defenestrate," Mrs. Darlingson said, reading his first word off the screen. "Very nice. Listen, Crow, your father and I were talking last night. You're growing up, in your own special way, and I can't stop that. I don't want to. Of course, this doesn't excuse your sneaking out, but if you like, today we can move the computer back up to your room."

"What about the lock on my door?"

She frowned. "Well, taking it off seems like a lot

of unnecessary work, but I'll promise not to lock you in—unless you give me a reason."

This was good. Really good. Crow tried to feel happy, but something nagged at him. Returning the computer to his room meant going back to the way things used to be. And things used to be awfully lonely.

"What about Melody? Can I see her again?"

Mrs. Darlingson tousled the clumps of hair on Crow's head. "I suppose you could invite her over sometime. I could fix dinner."

"Really?"

"Well, if you don't want to, that's fine. It was just an idea. Your father's idea, actually, not that he'll be the one to cook for—"

"No!" Crow interrupted. "I mean, yes. I want her to come over. I'll email her right now."

"There's no rush," Mrs. Darlingson said, and she went in the kitchen to get her morning cup of coffee.

Crow kept checking his email for Melody's reply. It finally came that evening.

Their late night had landed her in trouble, just as Crow had predicted. She had to spend Sunday in her bedroom. She also had to do extra chores for the next three months, and she was never allowed to hang out with Grace, Hannah, Luke, or Travis again—Mr. Plympton still thought she'd gone trick-or-treating with them.

He also thought that they were to blame for the times Melody and Crow had sneaked out back in early October. They'd pressured Crow and Melody into going to the park, Melody had convinced him, and Crow had been against it from the start. She also told her father that Crow's skin problems came from complications related to chicken pox, a virus she was fully vaccinated against, so there was nothing to worry about.

She'd done a lot of lying. But it was for a good cause, Crow thought, so maybe it was okay.

She promised to come over for dinner Monday night.

The email didn't mention anything about the wish until the very end. *There's more magic than I realized. I can't get away from it.*

Mrs. Darlingson prepared a pot roast. As the smell wafted through the house, Crow wondered if perhaps he'd made the wrong wish after all. Sure, a selfish wish would have caused him to fail the last test, but if it meant he could have pot roast, it might have been worth it.

And Luke really hadn't deserved his help. He knew that now, after what his father had told him.

Melody came as promised. She wore what was, for her, a normal outfit: blue-and-green-checkered leggings and a pink sweater decorated with purple pompoms. But she had pinned a bouquet of herbs to her sweater, which was strange even for her. Her skin glistened as if coated in oil.

"I'm so glad you were finally able to make it over," Mrs. Darlingson said, though Crow thought it sounded a little forced. "Dinner's almost ready. Why don't you have a seat?"

Crow and Melody sat down at the dinner table while Mrs. Darlingson went into the kitchen.

"I'm glad your dad doesn't hate me anymore," Crow said.

"Yeah. Now he hates Grace and Hannah. They weren't at school today. Travis, either."

Melody's pupils darted back and forth as she spoke, tracking something Crow couldn't see. Every once in a while, she jumped a little.

"How's your wish going?"

"Huh? Oh. Not as well as I'd expected." She jerked her head. "Did you see that?"

"See what?"

"Never mind. It's gone. Luke avoided me today, which seemed pretty ungrateful if you ask me. He's fine except his hands are still burned. Everyone thinks he hurt himself with the firecrackers—Okay, you have to see that. It's right on your nose!"

Crow frowned. Even crossing his eyes, he couldn't see anything on his nose. Couldn't feel anything, either, not even when he poked his nose with his finger.

Melody took a small jar out of her pocket. It contained oil with green, purple, and black specks in it, which she daubed on her neck. "Want some? It'll protect you from magical dangers."

Crow noticed that she had specks all over her hair and skin. She must have been using that oil a lot. It smelled like basil. "No thanks."

Mrs. Darlingson walked in with dinner. "I hope you like it."

Crow was used to sitting idly by during meals, so despite how good the pot roast smelled, he didn't really mind. Melody, however, was not used to it at all, and she kept shooting him awkward glances—when she wasn't distracted by things no one else could see. As a result, she hardly ate anything at all.

"So Crow tells me the two of you have become rather good friends," Mrs. Darlingson said. "I hope you don't plan to share what you've learned about him. We like our privacy, you understand."

"She's not going to tell anyone," Crow said.

Melody had speared a green bean with her fork, but before she could take a bite, she put down the fork in order to shoo something away. "Crow's right. I'm good with secrets."

"I'm glad to hear that. How's school?"

"Okay," Melody said, looking up at the ceiling. She shuddered.

"Is there something wrong with the food? You're not a vegetarian, are you? Crow didn't mention anything. He should have told me if you were a vegetarian."

"Huh? No. It's good." She ate half her food in several large bites. "Delicious."

They ate in silence, and everything seemed fine until Melody jumped up from her seat. A small scream escaped her lips, and she threw her glass of water at the wall. The glass shattered into wet pieces.

"I don't know how your father raises you," Mrs. Darlingson said. "But around here, we refrain from breaking things if we can help it."

"Sorry. I saw—I thought I saw—" Melody ran out of the room.

Crow ran after her. "It's your wish, isn't it?"

She stopped in the middle of the living room, her face streaked with tears. "I doused myself with this mixture," she said, gesturing to the oily stuff that covered her skin and hair. "It repels magic, but not enough—things still come near me; they just avoid touching me. And it makes me look ridiculous—like I needed to give people at school another reason to laugh at me!"

Crow handed her a napkin, and she used it to wipe away her tears.

"I thought it would be great," she continued, "seeing magic everywhere, immediately understanding whatever I see. It should be wonderful, but it's not. There are creatures everywhere: sprites, elves, goblins, ogres, trolls, bugbears, things made completely out of fire. And wormholes, too. Entire dimensions are hidden all around us. And I've learned something. Magical creatures stay hidden for a reason. They don't like being seen. Imps—they're like fairies but even worse—have started following me around at school just because they know it bothers me. They keep making faces and rude gestures and threatening to cause trouble—knock things over, pinch people, stuff like that—so it looks like I did it. I can't concentrate on anything. I hate it."

"It was a test," Crow said. "The wish wasn't a reward. It was the final test. Selfish wishes always go wrong." He picked a maggot out of his ear. "That's why I'm the way I am."

"But your parents' wish wasn't selfish. They did it for you!"

"They did it for themselves, too, because they were sad. And there was another wish before that." He told her what his father had told him about his death.

Fresh tears pooled in her eyes. "It isn't fair. The Meera doesn't have the right to judge people like this."

"No, it doesn't. Do you think we could stop it?" He didn't know how, but they had to do *something*.

"You want to face the Meera again?" She wiped her tears away, looking so hopeful that Crow didn't have the heart to tell her that confronting the Meera was the last thing he wanted to do.

CHAPTER TWENTY

Crow cleaned up the shattered glass while Mrs. Darlingson washed the dishes.

"Can she come over for dinner again next week?" he asked.

Mrs. Darlingson frowned. "I don't know if I have enough glassware to have her over every week. Why don't we discuss this later? You wanted to watch that dinosaur documentary tonight, didn't you? I think it's starting soon."

To her, *later* meant *never*. Worrying that his situation might not change that much after all, Crow trudged into the living room. Sure, Melody had come over for dinner, and that had been great, aside from the glass breaking and the crying. But it had also been a one-time event. Things were already returning to normal.

He was back to being a prisoner in his own home, and now it felt even lonelier than before.

He watched the dinosaur documentary, though he didn't enjoy it as much as he once would have. Maybe he was getting too old for dinosaurs. He'd loved them when he was little, but that had been years ago. Did other kids his age still like them, or had they moved on—and if so, to what?

Crow's parents had wished for him to have the chance to grow up. He was beginning to realize that nobody—dead or alive—could do that all alone.

Tuesday morning, Crow studied by his window, where he could watch Melody waiting for the bus. Luke was there as well, but the two didn't talk much. Travis, Grace, and Hannah were not there. Melody had said they'd missed school on Monday, too, though she hadn't said why.

Crow rushed through his schoolwork—twenty algebra problems, an essay on the Qin dynasty of China, a chemistry experiment that involved measuring endothermic reactions, and the last thirty pages of *Gulliver's Travels*—in order to make sure he was done by the time Melody got back from school. She'd emailed him to say she'd be coming over again, if that was okay, which of course it was. With Crow, anyway. He hadn't mentioned it to his mother.

When the doorbell rang, Mrs. Darlingson frowned

and sighed and shooed Crow into the shadows before answering the door.

"Oh, Melody, if you're here to apologize about the broken glass, there's really no need."

"Sorry about that." She waved to Crow. "Hi."

Crow stepped out of the shadows. "Hi, Melody. Uh, Mom, we're going outside." He raced to the backyard, with Melody close behind, before Mrs. Darlingson could stop them. They sat down on the ground. "Do you think you could use magic to help me? You know, make me alive, or at least seem more alive."

"No. Sorry. That was one of the first things I thought of, but there really isn't anything I can do. At least, not that I can find. I haven't had any luck figuring out what happened to my mom, either. I don't actually understand magic until I see it with my own eyes, and that usually only happens when something magical is messing with me." She threw a rock at the fence; Crow wasn't sure whether she was throwing it randomly or aiming at some magical nuisance. "This wish is awful."

"Is it getting any better?"

"No." She looked even worse than she had the day before, her eyes swollen and bloodshot. "I haven't been able to sleep."

"Can you tell me about what you see?" Crow asked. Maybe if he understood more, he'd be in a better position to help.

"Well, I always suspected that we were surrounded

by magic, but there's even more of it than I thought. It doesn't come from here, though. On its own, this world doesn't have a lick of magic." She pushed her finger through the magic-free dirt. "There are other worlds, magical universes, and sometimes a passageway opens up between them, like when lightning strikes a place where the separation of the universes is weak."

"Is that where the Meera comes from? A magical universe?" If so, it didn't seem like a place Crow would ever want to visit—an entire world filled with monsters like the Meera.

Melody frowned. "No, the Meera is different. It was created. You know that collar around its neck? It's dragon bone, not metal, and the inscriptions are in the fairy language. Someone put that on a regular animal to turn it into a shape-shifting chimera. It's a bunch of animals all combined, including magical ones, which is why it's so powerful."

"Why would anyone want to do that?"

"I'm not sure. Maybe just to see if it could be done. Maybe they thought they could control the monster. Or maybe—Oh! Can we move? There's an earth spirit underneath us, and I think we're annoying her. If we don't move, she'll probably start biting us. It happens a lot, although most people mistake the bites for bug bites."

Crow looked around but didn't see anything. He followed Melody to the other side of the yard, though.

When they were seated again, Melody continued. "It's horrible, but some people hunt creatures for their magical parts. Unicorn horns, dragon tears, manticore venom, that sort of thing. See, humans don't have any magical powers on their own, so it's the only way they can manage powerful spells." She winced. "It's possible someone created the Meera as a way to harvest a bunch of magical ingredients at once. And then, I don't know, I guess the Meera escaped."

That would explain the Meera's hatred of humans. It was pretty unfair, though. Crow and Melody had never tried to hunt a unicorn for its horn. "How do you know all this?"

"It's kind of hard to explain. After the wish, when I looked at the Meera's collar, I just saw it. I understood it. It's not as great as I'd thought, though. For one thing, being able to understand magic isn't that useful. I can't actually control it. Although I did figure out how to lure a brownie to my room." She saw the confused look on Crow's face and smiled. "The elf, not the dessert. Brownies are helpful elves that'll do anything for honey. As long as I keep feeding it, I'll never need to clean my room again. I think I might even be able to get it to do my homework. It answered some of my questions about things I couldn't see, too."

"That sounds great! See, it's not so bad. And what about that potion you made?"

She took the vial of the oily concoction out of her pocket. "You mean this? Some stuff in our world repels magic. I mixed together as much as I could get my hands on—castor oil, salt, pepper, iron from iron supplements, and basil—but it's still pretty weak. Magical creatures don't like to touch it because it weakens their magic, but it doesn't stop them from getting close. They're everywhere!" She buried her face in her hands and started sobbing. "It's awful. I can't get a break from them at all."

Crow patted her gently on her back, careful not to touch any part of her shirt that was obviously coated in oil. The mixture was supposed to repel magic. What if it repelled the magic keeping him alive?

Melody sniffled. She had wanted to see magic so desperately. Why, then, did seeing a little more than she had anticipated make her so miserable? The earth spirits and imps couldn't be that bad, and the brownie sounded wonderful. Crow thought she should be happy, but he also knew why she couldn't be.

The Meera punished selfish desires like hers. It had found a way to twist her wish. And if it had the power to alter her mind so that she could understand magic, surely it had the power to make her tormented by it, too.

He'd wanted to help her, but he didn't see how he could undo the curse, especially if humans couldn't wield magic. The best he could do was try to cheer her up. "Some of what you see must be neat, though, like the brownie. Can you show me anything?"

She removed her face from her hands and wiped her tears away. "You won't be able to see most things."

"Most things? So there are some things I can see?"

She pressed her lips together as she thought. "Well, there's that earth elemental over there. You can't see her directly, but I might get her to do something you can see." Melody stood up and began gathering rocks, which wasn't too hard since the yard contained little else. She took the collection to where they had been sitting and stacked one rock on top of the other. "Turn around now. If you're looking, she won't do it."

Crow wasn't sure what the earth elemental was supposed to do, but he followed Melody's instructions and turned around.

"Okay, now look."

Crow looked. Instead of a stack of two rocks, there was a stack of three. Melody added a fourth rock, and after they turned around for a few moments again, they found that a fifth rock had been added.

"Earth elementals love stacking rocks," Melody explained. "In some areas, there are stacks like this everywhere. That means there are a lot of elementals around."

Crow smiled as widely as his dead muscles would allow. "That's really cool! See, your wish isn't all bad."

Melody started to smile, too. Then she screamed.

"What's wrong?" Crow asked.

"There are gnomes here. The earth elemental is attracting them."

Crow searched the yard, but of course he couldn't spot them. "Are gnomes dangerous?"

"Not if you ignore them. But how can I ignore them when I can see them?" She took out her vial and dabbed herself with more of the magic-repelling oil.

Melody shrieked as something small and thin struck her shoulder. To Crow, it seemed to have come from nowhere. He plucked it from Melody's shirt. It looked like a cactus needle. "Did the gnomes do that?"

Melody nodded as another one hit her leg. "They use needles and thorns as darts. Don't look over there or they'll think you can see them, too. They don't like being seen." More cactus needles rained down on her. "I'm sorry. I can't stop them. I have to go."

When the doorbell rang the following afternoon, Mrs. Darlingson made only a cursory attempt to hide Crow before answering the door. "Hello, Melody." She looked at the boy accompanying Melody. "Who are you?"

"Luke."

"Luke Ebsworth?" Her face soured, like the name left a bad taste in her mouth. "What are you doing here?"

Crow was wondering the same thing. Melody wasn't allowed to hang out with Luke anymore, and even though she probably wouldn't get caught while her father was still at work, she must have had a pretty good reason to take the risk.

"We need to talk to Crow," Melody said. She stepped inside, pushing past Mrs. Darlingson. Because she was holding on to Luke's sleeve, he came in, too.

"He's busy," Mrs. Darlingson said, her eyes tracking Luke. "Melody, why don't you come over later?"

Crow stepped between his mother and his guests. "It's okay. I'm not busy." Quickly so his mother wouldn't have time to protest, he led them to the backyard.

Melody still had Luke by the shirt, practically dragging him the entire way. "Tell Crow what you told me."

He jerked his arm to free himself from Melody's grip. "The monster might've gone back for Travis, Grace, and Hannah on Halloween night. The three of them might still be stuck in the other glass cases."

"They might be? What do you mean? What makes you think that?" Crow asked.

Luke was silent until Melody punched his shoulder. "Well, when I was in the case, I couldn't move, but I could still see and hear what was going on. I kind of saw the monster throw them into the other cases and cover them with those black sheets."

The words took a while to settle in Crow's mind. The Meera had been holding Luke's friends captive for almost four days, and Luke had known the entire time. "Why didn't you tell us immediately?"

Luke opened his mouth but shut it again without saying anything. The smugness disappeared from his face. He looked down at his feet, and when he finally spoke, his voice came out soft and uncertain. "I wanted to, but that monster was howling, and I—I was—I was scared."

So much so that he deserted his friends? Friends he didn't even realize he was lucky to have? Crow wanted to yell at Luke, but he stopped himself. The Meera was the enemy here. And the howling had been pretty horrible.

Crow patted Luke's arm. "It's okay. Everyone gets scared sometimes."

"Some people more than others," Melody mumbled.

Luke shook Crow's hand—and the maggots that went with it—away. "I thought the monster would let them go, but it's been a couple of days, and nobody's seen them. People keep asking me where they are, and I think they know I'm lying when I say I don't know."

"Their parents have put up signs all around the neighborhood, and the police were at school asking questions today," Melody said.

Crow hadn't heard anything, but he hadn't been watching the news recently. He'd been too busy rushing through his homework so he'd have time to spend with Melody.

"We need to tell someone," Luke said. "Not about that monster. Nobody would believe that. But I can tell my dad there's somebody living under the park, some creep who took them. My dad can organize a rescue party."

"Your dad already knows about the monster," Crow said.

Luke looked confused. "How?"

"It doesn't matter," Melody said. "He still won't know how to handle the Meera. It's powerful. If it sees a bunch of men—police with weapons—coming down into its territory, it'll attack. It'll win."

"So what do you want to do?" Crow asked.

"We need to go back." She didn't look any better than she had the night before. Her eyes were still red and puffy, her skin ashen. Things nobody else could see still distracted her. "We can rescue them. And we can stop the Meera once and for all. I think."

After sitting down carefully to pick a place uninhabited by elementals or gnomes, she told Crow and Luke her plan.

When Melody finished, Crow and Luke sat in silence.

The silence stretched on a little too long, but Crow couldn't think of what to say.

"What do you think?" Melody asked.

"It's risky."

"But it'll work. We'll both get what we want, for real this time. Think of what that will mean for you. And we can't just leave Travis, Grace, and Hannah there, can we? I think we should do it. Now. I can grab the supplies on the way."

"I'm in," Luke said. "They're my friends."

Crow glanced at the kitchen window, where Mrs. Darlingson watched him while pretending to do the dishes. "I'm in, too. But not yet. I need to do something first. We can meet at the park in an hour." He hesitated. "Melody, maybe you could take a nap in the meantime."

"Doubtful. I used to think that the whole monster-under-the-bed thing was a myth, but it's actually true, you know. They don't want to hurt anyone—they just feed off people's dreams—but having one of those things there, right under me, is still creepy." She shuddered. "I don't think I'll ever sleep again. Not unless we pull this off."

After Melody and Luke left, Crow went inside. He needed to tell his mother something, but he hadn't decided what. He ended up staring at her awkwardly.

She sighed. "I know things have been difficult for you ever since—ever since—well, you know." She left the mug she'd been washing for the last fifteen minutes in the sink, and they sat down at the table. "I'm glad that Melody's coming over."

"You are?" Maybe he'd heard that wrong. He checked his ears for maggots.

"Of course. She makes you happy; I see that. You have to understand that I just want to protect you. I love you. But your father's right. You're growing up, and I can't keep you locked away in your room forever. If you want to be friends with Melody, or even Luke"—her face soured again—"you can."

"I don't want to be friends with Luke," Crow said.

"Oh, thank goodness. Why don't you go up to your room and draw? Or we can play a game, if you'd like."

"Okay, but can I go out later? Melody wants me to meet her."

"Today? Really? She was just over here." She forced a smile. "I suppose that's fine. But, Crow, you need to be careful. Other people won't understand you. They might even try to hurt you. Promise me you'll be careful?"

Crow nodded. "I promise." And he meant it, too, but he also knew that all the care in the world couldn't make what he was planning safe.

CHAPTER TWENTY-ONE

At Mrs. Darlingson's insistence, Crow wore an oversized hooded sweatshirt, hood up. Gloves, too. The evening was a little chilly, so the warm clothes wouldn't look too conspicuous, and they would help hide his state of decay from any passersby.

As Crow walked to the park, the wind blew in a thick layer of gray clouds. A light sprinkling of rain became a heavy downpour, and the streets emptied as everyone hurried inside their warm, dry homes. When Crow reached the park, he found it empty—except for Melody.

"Have you been waiting long?" he asked. Her duckling-decorated raincoat kept the top half of her dry, but her red-and-green velvet pants were soaked, and the rain had washed the protective oil from her hair.

"Not too long. Luke's not here yet." Her eyes widened in horror. "Wait! Don't move!"

Crow stopped with one foot in midair.

"There's a fairy trap right in front of you. Don't you see it?"

Crow shook his head. With all the rain, he couldn't see much of anything, although he doubted that he'd be able to see a fairy trap, whatever that was, on even the sunniest of days. "What do I do?"

"Come this way." She guided him around the hazard.

"Thanks. What would have happened to me if I'd stepped on it?"

"A bad case of the hiccups." She smiled, something she hadn't done much since Halloween. "Okay, so maybe it wasn't exactly life and death. Fairies leave traps like that everywhere. Some make you hiccup, like this one. Others make you sneeze, or forget what you were doing, or get a really bad itch right on that part of your back you can't reach. One unties your shoelaces. They think it's funny."

"What about kidnappings?" Crow asked. "Do fairies think that's funny, too?"

"You're asking if they could have taken my mother, right?" Melody pressed her lips into a thin line. "I don't know. It's possible."

"Where are the fairies?" He looked around. If they

caught one, maybe they could ask it. Force it to talk, if necessary. Not that Crow knew how he'd go about forcing a fairy to talk, but he'd figure it out if it meant finding Melody's mother.

"They're not here anymore. Too wet. They'll come out once the storm's over—which makes them smarter than us right now. Let's go to the shed. The Meera might curse us, or lock us up forever, but at least we'll get out of this rain."

"But we can't! Not yet! Once it's done, you won't be able to talk to the fairies." His voice became a whisper. "You won't be able to find your mom."

"It's okay. You remember that brownie I told you about?" Crow nodded, and she continued. "I gave it a jar of honey and asked it to find my mother. It's out there right now, looking for her, so I don't need to talk to fairies."

"What about Luke? He'll be here any minute."

"Do you really want to wait for him? He didn't help last time."

Crow couldn't deny that. Still, ditching him didn't seem right. "He might be better this time."

"I doubt it. He's probably not even coming. I bet he chickened out again. Or he decided to tell his father, and soon we'll have an angry mob on our hands. Our best chance is if we go now, just the two of us."

"Okay," Crow said. Melody's wish had made her the expert when it came to magical problems. He had to trust that she knew what she was doing—otherwise they were doomed.

In the shed, the Meera neither cursed them nor took them prisoner. It didn't even show up, at least not as far as Crow could tell—although it was dark enough that something could have been hiding right beside them. He didn't hear anything, but he didn't think he would have been able to hear the Meera if it had taken the form of something small: a mouse lurking in the corner, or a cockroach resting in a crevice.

Melody removed two flashlights from the backpack she'd been carrying. She handed one to Crow, and they looked around the shed. There was nothing there, not even a fly.

Crow pointed to her backpack. "You have everything we'll need? The ne—"

"It might be listening," Melody interrupted. "But yes, I have everything."

She pushed against the wall. "The shortcut's right here. This is where we came out after the Meera granted our wishes. The magical passageway's still here, but it's locked with a spell from this side. I can't open it. We'll have to use the grate again."

Crow pulled up the metal grate and jumped down. Melody followed.

The hall was exactly as it had been before— endless and decorated with tortoise engravings. They began walking.

"The hall does loop," Melody said. "It just doesn't loop in a circle like you'd expect. Space-time loops, folding reality in on itself."

Crow nodded thoughtfully. He'd read that space-time could curve, and he knew that some scientists thought wormholes might connect one place to another, but he'd never expected to experience the theoretical physics firsthand. "Is there any way to unfold it?"

"Yes, but I can't do it." She sighed. "One of the many reasons why this wish isn't so great. Understanding magic isn't the same as being able to use magic." She touched the strap of her backpack. "Although it does help a little."

She determined that the fastest way through the test was to walk slowly but steadily, without taking any breaks. Crow expected the mud to appear any second. He steeled himself in anticipation. They got through it once, so they could get through it again.

But the mud never appeared.

"Is the path getting steeper?" he asked. He slowed down in order to inspect the incline.

Melody yanked him forward. "We have to keep going. But yes, it's getting steeper."

After a little while, the slant became obvious. Before, the hall had been perfectly flat as far as Crow could tell, but now it was like climbing up a mountain. If it got much steeper, they would need rock-climbing equipment.

The ground shook.

"Look out!" Crow screamed as a boulder rolled toward them.

There was nowhere to move. The large rock was nearly as wide as the hall, so even pressing themselves against the walls wouldn't help. Maybe they could try to jump over the boulder, but since it was nearly as tall as they were, success seemed incredibly unlikely.

They were going to be flattened.

Crow couldn't stand to see his best friend—his only friend—get squashed. He closed his eyes.

No pain came, but that wasn't surprising. His dead nerves couldn't feel much of anything. He wondered whether the rock had already rolled over him.

"It's okay," Melody said.

Crow opened his eyes. The boulder had stopped a few feet in front of him, though he didn't see how. The steep incline meant that it should have tumbled right over them.

"There's a magical barrier," Melody explained. "We can pass it, but the rock can't. I'm not sure what we're supposed to do now, though. Maybe we can go over it."

She tried to climb over the boulder, but it was too round, too smooth. She kept slipping off.

"We have to push it," Crow said. "Like Sisyphus."

"Sisyphus? Is that a type of rock?"

"No, he's a king from Greek mythology. The gods punished him by making him push a boulder up a hill.

When he reached the top, the boulder would slide back down, and he'd have to push it up again."

"How long did he have to do that for?"

Crow hesitated. "Eternity, I think."

"That doesn't sound very promising," Melody said, though she started pushing against the boulder anyway.

It was heavy, but not as heavy as Crow had expected. Working together, they forced it to budge inch by inch. Sweat dripped down Melody's forehead, and Crow wondered whether they should have waited for Luke after all. Of the three of them, he was definitely the strongest.

The inches became yards.

The boulder wobbled. Melody whimpered.

"What's wrong?" Crow asked. They'd stopped moving forward, but keeping the boulder in place still required a lot of effort.

"My shoe came untied a while ago, and now it's slipping off. It's making it hard to walk."

"Fix it."

Melody turned to her side. Leaning against the rock, she raised her foot and adjusted her sneaker.

The boulder shook as it pushed against Crow's palms. Melody must have felt it, too, because she stopped tying her laces.

"Run!" Crow yelled. They couldn't stop it. The boulder was rolling down the hill.

The slope ensured that, once the boulder started moving, it moved quickly. It also made running difficult. Melody and Crow stumbled, and within seconds they were tumbling down the hill, the large rock a hair's width away from crushing them.

Then the boulder stopped. They'd passed the magical barrier.

It took them a while to stop tumbling.

Melody didn't bother standing up. "Let's take a break before we try again." She tied her sneakers, checking that both laces were tight. Then she got some water and a chocolate bar out of her bag.

"The Meera said the tests would be harder the second time," Crow said. It must have known that they would come for Grace, Hannah, and Travis. Hopefully it didn't realize their other reason for returning.

Melody didn't respond. She was too busy chugging her water.

After a while, she stood up, and they tried again. It wasn't any easier. With every step, they faced the possibility that they would stumble, that Melody's sweaty hands would slip, or that Crow's atrophied muscles would give out, and the boulder would crush them.

Melody grunted and wheezed. Crow was pushing as hard as he could, but he suspected that she was doing most of the work. He just couldn't get his dead body to do any better.

"I need to stop," Melody panted.

"We can't." They'd be crushed. Even if they somehow survived, they'd have failed the test. The Meera would curse them. Again.

"I just need a break."

"One more step," Crow said. She took a step, a tiny one, and he repeated his encouragement. "One more step. One more step."

He couldn't help worrying that, like Sisyphus, they'd be stuck doing this for eternity. But then the boulder disappeared, its oppressive weight vanishing with it.

A door appeared in front of them. They had passed the test.

The next room had the crow engravings, but little else remained the same. For one thing, the giant birdbath was missing. The exit was different, too. This time, it wasn't high up in a spot that could be reached only by scaling the wall. Instead, it was right in front of them, as easy to reach as could be.

Unfortunately, there wasn't one exit. There were many.

Melody sat down. "I'm so glad we don't have to climb like last time. I don't think I could after that."

"See anything to help us figure out which door to use?" Crow asked.

Melody shook her head. "Whatever the solution is, it doesn't involve magic. I guess we should just try one."

She got up and pulled on one of the doors, but it didn't budge. She tried another and another, and Crow did the same, but they were all locked.

"Come over here," Melody said. She was standing in the center of the room, where thin lines in the floor hinted at a secret opening. Her fingers fought to pry the cover open, but with no success.

One spot in the middle of the lines seemed darker than the rest. Crow pushed at it, and a piece of the floor slid back to reveal a secret hollow.

Inside sat a pyramid-shaped box. A tetrahedron, Crow thought, remembering the shape from one of his geometry lessons. Each corner of the four triangular sides bore a picture of an animal or a plant.

Melody picked it up. "Look, it opens."

She slid one part of one side off to reveal a space much smaller than the large box suggested. Inside was a key. She rushed forward to the doors, trying the key in each. On her fourth try, the key fit, and the door opened.

"We did it! That was fast!"

Something buzzed.

"Close the door!" Crow yelled.

Melody screamed as a large colony of bees flew

toward her. She jerked left, then right, then back, her screams intensifying.

Crow rushed toward the door. He slammed it shut in time to keep most, but not all, of the bees out. Those that had made it inside buzzed around aimlessly.

Lumps swelled on Melody's forehead and on both her arms. "Are you allergic?" Crow asked. She shook her head. Using what little fingernails he had left, Crow helped her remove the stingers. He took care not to squeeze them, which would cause them to release more of their venom into her skin.

Once he was sure Melody was okay, he returned his attention to the tetrahedron. "The sides move," he said, demonstrating how each part could twist around. With each new formation, a different part slid off to reveal a different key. "How do we know which key is right?" After the bee incident, trying the doors at random seemed like a very dangerous idea.

"The pictures must have something to do with it," Melody said.

Crow studied them: a big fish, a small fish, a snake, a coyote, a frog, an otter, a rabbit, a mouse, a fly, grass, acorns, and a green blob. He couldn't quite tell what the last one was supposed to depict. The tetrahedron shape meant that three pictures always came together at each of the four vertices. "Maybe we're supposed to put the animals into groups."

Thinking that the green blob could be some sort of plant, he wanted to put the acorn, the grass, and the green blob together, but the acorn and the blob were on the same side, so putting them together was impossible. He twisted the sides so that the two fish were together, but there wasn't another fish to complete the group. He thought maybe the frog would work, but that put the fly and the acorn together, and he didn't see how that made sense.

Melody and Crow spent the next hour or so passing the tetrahedron back and forth. They tried many combinations, but none of them quite made sense.

Melody threw the tetrahedron on the floor. "We could just try the doors. If we peek through first, we'll be okay."

Crow picked up the tetrahedron. "The other doors might contain things that are worse than bees. And the danger might not be obvious at first. We could walk out, seeing nothing and thinking we're fine, and then get mauled by a bear."

So they kept twisting the sides in search of a combination that made sense.

After suggesting that they go by color and size, Melody offered one more idea: "What about the food chain?"

Crow looked at the tetrahedron again. The rabbit would eat the grass, and the coyote would eat the rabbit. The snake would eat the mouse, which would eat the acorns. The otter would eat the fish, but also the frog, which would eat the fly. The big fish would eat the small fish, and the small fish would eat . . . algae! That was what the green blob was.

After Melody had twisted all of the sides into the right position, a part of one side slid off to reveal a key.

"Stay back." Crow wanted Melody to be as far away as possible in case this combination was wrong and something even worse than bees attacked.

But when Crow opened the door, nothing attacked. The door opened to a well-lit hall. They had passed another test.

CHAPTER TWENTY-TWO

Without taking a break, they headed to the next room. Crow rubbed his wrist, where a line of stitches was all that kept his hand attached.

"Maybe your wish will help us with the next test," Crow said, doing his best to sound cheerful. "It has to come in handy sometimes."

Melody scowled. "You've clearly never had to learn math from a werewolf. Every time I see him, I want to scream or offer him a dog treat, but I'm pretty sure he'd fail me if I did anything like that."

"Your math teacher is a werewolf? Didn't you notice that before?"

"No. He looks more or less normal most of the time—unless you understand all forms of magic, that is. It was much better when I thought he was a regular, although somewhat hairy, human."

"Are there any other monsters at your school?" Crow asked. "What about the librarian? Is she really an alien like you thought?"

Melody frowned. "The librarian seems normal— although I don't think I could detect alien technology, assuming it was based in science, not magic. The history teacher isn't really a warlock, either, and if the school food's being poisoned, it's not with anything magical, and nobody's gotten sick anyway, so I guess I was wrong about that, too. There are things I hadn't noticed before, though: the werewolf and two sisters who are half elf. Really, you'd fit in at the school pretty well just the way you are."

"You've clearly never had to remove a maggot from your nose. Unlike your math teacher, I can't exactly pass for normal."

The room looked more or less as they remembered it, with engravings of dogs on the walls and two dark areas on either side of the torch-lit center.

"Don't step there," she said, pointing to where Crow was about to put his foot. "Come this way. Now jump." And like that, she led him through the magical minefield. No swords swung at them. No arrows whizzed past. No guillotines chopped off their hands. It was the easiest test yet.

"Look out!" Crow shoved Melody out of the way as two fireballs zoomed toward them.

The fireballs chased them. Like before, one pushed Crow to the right, while Melody's fireball forced her to the left. This time, though, his dream room did not greet him.

This area had no torches. He still had his flashlight, as well as the flickering light of the fireball, and he used both to examine the dark area. Other than two large buttons, the writing on which Crow couldn't quite make out from where he stood, there wasn't much of anything. At least there weren't any spiders.

A previously unseen door thudded shut, trapping Crow inside. The fireball grew larger and larger and larger. It threatened to fill the entire space.

Crow squeezed around the growing fireball in order to examine the two buttons. The writing on one said, "Burn left side. Extinguish right side." The other one bore a similar but reversed message: "Burn right side. Extinguish left side."

The right side, where he'd been chased, or the left side, where Melody had been chased.

The first time Crow went through this test, the Meera demanded that he sacrifice his dreams in order to save Melody and demonstrate his loyalty. This time, the Meera required him to sacrifice his life.

They should have known better than to try to trick the Meera.

Crow couldn't see Melody now that the door had shut, but he knew she must be similarly trapped. He had to act quickly, before she had a chance to decide which button of hers to press.

Burn right side. Extinguish left side. He'd barely been alive anyway. And he wouldn't be able to feel the pain.

He pushed the button and waited for the flames.

But the flames never came. The fireball extinguished itself. The door swooshed open.

Crow ran to meet Melody, who was running to meet him. She flung her arms around Crow. "You figured it out!"

"Figured what out?" Crow asked, surprised by the hug. He couldn't remember the last time anyone had hugged him, really hugged him. Even his mother favored a quick pat on the back or a gentle squeeze to anything resembling an actual embrace. And his father—well, his father hadn't been much of a hugger *before* Crow became an undead thing.

"You know. Of course you know." Melody pulled back with only a slight twitch of her nose and a very subtle flick of her hands to brush off any stray maggots. "As long as we both chose to be loyal, to extinguish the other side and sacrifice our own, nobody would get hurt."

Oh. That made sense. "Uh, yeah. I figured it out. Did your wish help you figure it out?"

She nodded. "Finally. I was beginning to think it would be no use at all. Let's hurry."

They entered the large, cavelike room with the honey badger engravings. Crow walked to the rickety bridge with no handrails. "I guess the Meera thought this test was bad enough that it didn't need to be changed. I don't suppose your wish can help us out here."

Melody looked down at the abyss. "It's not as deep as it looks. I mean, it doesn't go down forever and ever. Still, if we fall, it'll be bad. Broken limbs and stuff."

She placed one foot gingerly onto the bridge, which swayed and creaked in response. With even more care, she placed her other foot onto the bridge. It swung even more, almost bucking her off.

"Fearlessness," she said, and she ran full speed ahead. The bridge didn't sway; it barely even moved. Seconds later, she was safe and sound on the other side of the chasm.

"Come on!" she yelled. "As fast as you can."

"Are you sure?" Crow yelled back. Scooting across, like they had last time, seemed so much safer. Although the bridge had been more stable when she ran. And he did trust her. Nevertheless, his feet stayed firmly in place, refusing to move.

"A spell makes it sway more the slower you go!" Melody yelled. "Run!"

He took a big gulp of air—which was silly, really, since he didn't need to breathe—and ran. As he ran, a horrible thought occurred to him: what if he couldn't run fast enough? He wasn't much of an athlete. The bridge would sway, unimpressed with his sluggish speed, and he'd be thrown off. But by the time fear clamped down on him, he was already across. He'd done it.

The feeling of dread didn't leave, though. The second chasm—the one without any bridge at all—still awaited them.

This time, it was worse. Impossibly so, in fact, because the chasm didn't end. The gap extended all the way to the far wall, with no ledge for them to land on even if they were able to jump that far. Crow shined the flashlight down into the opening, which was filled with thick black bubbling goo.

"It's a tar pit," he said. "They're naturally occurring pools of asphalt. Paleontologists have found lots of fossils in them because any animal that enters one gets stuck and dies." Crow did not want to become one of those fossils.

Melody shook her head. "It's an illusion. There's no tar."

"Great! We can just walk across, right?"

"No. The tar's an illusion, but the chasm is real, and there's no bridge." She took a deep breath. "I think we have to be brave. I think we have to jump."

"Into what? What's down there?" It sure looked like a bubbling pool of asphalt to Crow.

"I don't know. I can tell that the tar is not actually there, but I don't know what it's covering. I guess we'll find out when we get there."

"But it could be anything. For all we know, the fake tar pit is hiding a real tar pit. Or there could be snakes, or lava, or something even worse."

"That's where the bravery comes in."

Crow wanted to point out that leaping into the unknown struck him as more foolish than brave. No one got a second wish. Maybe this test—this death trap—was how the Meera kept it that way. But before he could get the words out, Melody had jumped.

Crow kept his flashlight shined on her until the tar swallowed her. He waited a moment before deciding he had no choice but to follow. He jumped.

The tar disappeared the second it should have touched him, replaced by dark nothing. He seemed to fall for a very long time. He had time to spin upside down, and time to right himself. He had more than enough time to conclude that, when he finally hit the ground, he would do so with a splat that even he could not survive. He also had plenty of time to think about his mother and his father and how they would never know what had happened to him.

But when the ground finally came, it did so with a soft bounce.

"I couldn't see it from the top," Melody explained, "but there's a magic protection spell here." She fell backward, letting the magically softened ground cushion her.

The tortoise, the crow, the dog, and the honey badger—four tests down, and only three to go. Nevertheless, Crow was pretty sure the hardest part still lay ahead of them.

CHAPTER TWENTY-THREE

Next came the elephant room. They pulled the black sheet off the first glass case they came to, and just as Luke had promised, there was someone inside. She had bright blue eyes, matched perfectly by her blue dress. A diamond tiara sat atop her blond hair. A diamond necklace hung around her neck.

Her head was held high in an expression of contempt, but her eyes, which blinked occasionally, were full of fear.

Her case had a donation box, just like Luke's. A sign sat above it.

HANNAH SCHUSTER

It looks harmless, but this primate is vicious. If
it is not the center of attention, it will go mad

**with rage and attack any creature in sight. For
your own safety, stay far away.**

"Did you ever figure out what the elephant room
tests?" Melody asked.

"No." Crow had been too focused on the meaning of
the bees to give it much thought.

"Maybe we should leave them. I mean, just for now.
We can come back for them after we've dealt with the
Meera."

Crow looked at Hannah. She couldn't say anything,
but she could hear everything—Luke had been able
to. She knew they were talking about her. How would
she feel if they left her? Besides, they didn't know
what would happen when they faced the Meera. What
if they couldn't come back?

They might be able to use her help, too. They sure
could have used Luke's strength when they were pushing that boulder.

"We have to get them now."

Melody sighed. "I knew you'd say that. And you're
right, I guess. I brought some junk from my house for
the donation." She unzipped her backpack a couple of
inches, wide enough for her hand to slip through, but
not wide enough for anyone watching to see inside.
Her hand fished around for a minute before retrieving
a hair clip. It was cheap and plastic, and it appeared to
be broken.

She put it inside the box. Nothing clicked.

Crow tried to open the door, but it didn't budge.

Inside the case, Hannah moved. "What's going on?"

"Hi, Hannah," Melody said. "This is Crow. We're here to rescue you. Uh, we just need to figure out how first." She frowned. "That should have worked. Do you think the Meera changed this test, too?"

"Maybe. Can't you use your wish to understand the magic involved?"

She looked at the box. "It's set to open when it receives a donation of great value. Are elephants supposed to be charitable or something?"

"I'm not sure. But that clasp on that clip was broken, right? And you called it junk."

"I guess." Melody stuck her hand back inside the backpack and retrieved a lollipop. "Candy worked last time. And I only have a few pieces of Halloween candy left, so it definitely has value."

She put the lollipop inside the donation box. Nothing happened. "Now what?"

"Hurry up!" Hannah yelled.

"Each of the tests has gotten harder," Crow said. "And you said the magic required something of great value. I think you need to donate more."

Melody frowned. "Fine. But this had better work." She added the rest of her Halloween haul—two small chocolate bars and a piece of licorice—to the donation.

The lock clicked open.

Hannah barreled her way out and flung her arms around Melody. "Thank you! I thought I'd be stuck in there forever."

She turned to Crow. Her arms went out, then quickly retracted. She wrinkled her nose in an all-too-familiar way. "Uh, thank you. I'd hug you, too, but . . . what's wrong with you?"

"Dead," Crow mumbled.

"Cursed," Melody added.

Hannah put her hands on her hips. "I'm not going to kiss him."

"Why would we want you to kiss him?" Melody asked.

"Uh, hello, princess here." She pointed to her tiara. "You want me to kiss him to undo his curse, right? It might work—I am related to royalty on my father's side—but I'm not going to do it. I don't just go around kissing strangers. Especially not disgusting ones. Wait—are you a stranger? You look familiar."

"We used to go to school together," Crow said.

"Oh. I'm still not kissing you."

Melody rolled her eyes. "Whatever. We don't want you to kiss him. We need to free Grace and Travis now."

Hannah raised her chin, making herself look a lot like she had when she'd been frozen in the case. "This is all Travis's fault. His and Luke's. Where is Luke?"

"He already got out," Crow said.

The Meera's growls echoed through the room. It

timed this, Crow realized. It wanted to scare the bravery and compassion out of people.

And it was working. Hannah's pretty blue eyes bulged at the sound, which had morphed into a hyena's cackle. "Can I go, too? Right now, while you help the others?"

"Try to escape if you want. Crow and I are going to get the others. Good luck getting out of here and facing the Meera on your own." Melody's brow furrowed. "Did your nose just get bigger?"

"What? No." Hannah felt her nose. "I don't think so. How could it?"

Crow thought he had seen it, too—a slight lengthening of the bridge, a minor widening of the nostrils. But there was no point in saying anything before he was sure, especially not when they had two more people to rescue. Crow removed the sheet from the next case.

This one held a cute girl with long brown hair and big brown eyes, both of which shined in the glow of the flashlight. She was wearing a flattering Greek dress, which she was stuck looking down at.

GRACE AGUILAR

A vain creature, this primate is at home anywhere with a mirror. When others are around, it eats water and the occasional

vegetable. When alone, its diet includes any
chocolate or sausage that is available, often
consumed together. Many consider it a type
of parasite.

Melody held her hand out. "Hannah, give me your
tiara."

"No! This thing cost me a month's allowance! It's
genuine cubic zirconia, you know."

"Then it'll make the perfect donation." Melody
ripped the tiara from Hannah's hair and put it into
Grace's donation box. The lock clicked open.

Grace pushed her way out of the glass cage, knocked
Melody over, and kicked Crow. "It's another monster!
Get him."

"I'm here to help you," Crow said, holding up his
hands to protect himself.

"You'd better watch out, monster. A friend's been
teaching me martial arts." She punched Crow in the
stomach.

"He's not a monster," Melody said, pulling herself
up. "He's just a little dead."

Grace kicked Crow again. "I'm pretty sure that
makes him a monster."

"Then he's a good monster," Melody said. "One
who's rescuing you."

While Crow checked himself for injuries and

found none, the princess and the goddess huddled together, whispers passing back and forth between them.

"Fine," Hannah said. "But keep him away from us. He stinks."

Melody's nostrils flared at the insult. She was clearly very angry, although Crow didn't know why. He did stink. No one could deny it, not even Melody.

"And let's get out of here," Grace added, her voice almost drowned out by the Meera's howls. "Now."

"We have to rescue Travis first," Hannah said. Her tone suggested that this was a major inconvenience.

"That's not fair! This is all Travis's fault, anyway. We should leave him here!" As Grace said this, a large wart appeared on the tip of her nose.

Hannah screamed, and her own nose grew larger. A lot larger. It was now twice its normal size, and growing bigger by the second.

"What's happening?" Grace demanded as more warts sprouted all over her face, and her formerly perfect teeth became crooked.

"You've been cursed," Crow said. "We should be able to reverse the effects when we confront the Meera. Hopefully. But first we have to get Travis."

They uncovered the last case, where Travis, still dressed in his pirate costume, stood with his arms out, elbows bent and muscles flexed.

TRAVIS KLING

This primate prefers to travel in packs as long as it can be the alpha male. It believes itself to be much stronger than it actually is and will handle most disputes through violence.

Melody yanked off one of Grace's earrings and dropped it in the donation box. The glass door opened and Travis unfroze, though he didn't stop flexing his muscles immediately. "What's going on?"

"The Meera—that's the monster you were torturing when you thought it was a helpless rabbit—kidnapped you as punishment," Melody said. "Now that we've rescued you, we need to leave."

"Rescued me?" he said, and his chest puffed out even as his legs still wobbled. "I didn't need rescuing. In another minute, I'd have broken that glass." He leaned against a wall for support. "Now that we're together, I should take the lead. I am, after all, the strongest of the group. I'll fight this mons—Hannah? Grace? Is that you? What's wrong with you?"

"Nothing," Hannah said, her nose roughly the size of a toucan's beak. Her ears had started growing, too. She tried to hide behind Grace, whose warts were still multiplying and whose eyebrows had become large and bushy. At the same time, Grace tried to hide behind Hannah. They went back and forth in a desperate dance, both trying to use the other as a shield, until finally they settled on huddling together with their hair and hands covering as much of themselves as they could manage.

"You're ugly," Travis said, laughing. He shrank about an inch, although he was laughing too hard to notice.

"They've been cursed by the Meera," Crow explained. "You have, too. We'll try to break the curses when we confront the Meera on our way out of here."

"Cursed?" He looked Crow up and down. "Is that what's wrong with you?"

Crow nodded.

"But I'm not cursed," Travis said, just as he shrank another two inches. This time, he noticed. "What's happening? Is the room getting bigger?"

Melody coughed, and Crow suspected that she was trying to cover a giggle.

"No," she said when she'd caught her breath. "You're getting smaller."

CHAPTER TWENTY-FOUR

Travis still insisted on leading the way. Since he was headed toward the spider room, this was fine with Crow and Melody. Grace and Hannah, both of whom now had bowed legs and humped backs, stayed in the back of the group. For the most part, they kept their eyes on the ground, but every once in a while they would sneak peeks at each other. Crow knew whenever this happened, even though the girls were behind him, because they shrieked each time.

"As leader," Travis said, having reached the end of the hall, "I think we should go through this door."

His pants, now far too large for him, fell to his ankles. He scrambled to pull them up.

Melody smirked. "Wise decision. I don't know how Crow and I managed without you last time."

"Well, you did have Luke with you, and he's usually my second-in-command." With one hand keeping his pants up, Travis reached up to the doorknob, now level with his head. He opened the door and stepped onto the rectangular platform inside. "It looks like we'll have to swim."

Melody grabbed him before he could jump into the deadly liquid. "Not so fast. That water's filled with flesh-eating fish." She plucked his skull-and-crossbones bandanna from off his head and dipped it into the water. Then she offered the bandanna, half-eaten, back to him.

"No thanks." He stepped away from her. "You can keep it. And I, uh, order you to build a bridge. As your leader."

By now, all five of them had crowded onto the rectangular platform, which started to move. The series of platforms no longer formed a passageway straight to the door on the other side of the spider room. Instead, the platforms were once again scattered, slowly sliding back and forth. Any step off them and into the surrounding pool would mean instant death—or, at the very least, instant severe pain and injury.

"We have to wait," Crow said. "There's nothing else we can do. Eventually the rectangles will line up and we'll be able to walk out easily."

"What about this?" Grace asked. Gray and small, a button blended into the platform's edge. Despite this,

Crow was certain that it hadn't been there last time. During the long hours spent waiting in the spider room, he would have noticed a button no matter how good the camouflage was.

"What does it do?" Hannah asked, pressing it.

"Stop that," Melody said. She sounded worried.

"Is magic involved?" Crow asked.

Melody nodded. "The button only makes things worse."

"No, it doesn't." With his tiny fingers, Travis pointed to the nearest platform, currently moving toward them. "It must control these rectangle things. Look, it's making that one come closer."

Hannah and Grace pressed the button madly.

"No, it's not," Melody said. "It doesn't affect the other platforms at all. But it does make this one smaller, so you'd better stop unless you want to become fish food."

Grace analyzed the platform from under her very bushy eyebrows, which now covered the top third of her face, while warts covered the rest. She seemed to have trouble seeing and had to use a warty hand to remove her long brows from her eyes. "It's not getting smaller."

"Yes, it is," Melody insisted. "Just very slowly. Slowly enough that you can't notice, but if you keep pressing the button like that, it'll add up. Stop."

"If it's happening too slowly to notice, how do you know?" Hannah asked, her voice very nasal.

"I just do. It's magic, and I understand magic."

Travis laughed. It came out very high-pitched, as if he'd been sucking on helium. "Like how you understood the librarian was an alien?"

Melody's face reddened. "No. It's real this time. The Meera granted my wish, and now I—Why am I explaining this to you? Just stop it!" She pushed her way between Hannah and Grace and covered the button with her hands. "Sit down and wait."

"Hey, I'm in charge here," Travis squeaked. He looked up at Melody, now more than twice as tall as he was. "We'll try and do it your way 'cause you did this before, but just till I say otherwise."

So they settled down for the long wait. Travis, still shrinking, sat in the middle. He looked like a pile of clothes with a small head sticking out.

Melody and Crow sat by the button, in case the others decided to try pressing it again. They tried to pass the time by playing hangman—Melody had come prepared for the long wait with some paper and a pen—but neither could get into the game.

Hannah and Grace claimed the opposite edge as their own. They sat there and whispered to each other. It might have been motion sickness, or maybe just another symptom of the curse, but their skin was taking on a greenish hue. Occasionally one would cry, and the other would offer a comforting hug or a pat on the shoulder, as long as it didn't mean looking at each other.

Crow considered saying something to them. After all, he knew what it was like to go from a normal-looking kid to a deformed atrocity because of a curse. Despite this, he couldn't think of anything cheerful to say. His life hadn't exactly improved after his own curse, even if he finally did have a friend again, and their victory against the Meera was far from certain.

When another panel came close, Travis stood, although he had shrunk so much that it hardly made a difference. "Let's go."

Melody and Crow shook their heads.

"Not yet," Melody said as the panel slid away. "We have to wait."

Travis sat back down, or maybe he just shrank some more—it was hard to tell. Either way, he didn't say anything else. Other than Grace and Hannah's whispered conversation and the swooshing of the panels, the room was quiet.

But not for long. After a while, Grace and Hannah's whispers grew louder. Angrier. Eventually, they morphed into shouts.

"You're the ugly one!" said Hannah, identifiable only by the princess dress she wore. Her face, all chin hair and nose, looked nothing like the beautiful visage Crow had seen on Halloween.

"If I'm uglier now," Grace said, "it's only because normally I'm the prettier one. That's why I've starred in commercials and you haven't." She, too, could be identified only by her costume. Her face, neck, and arms were completely covered in warts. Even her warts had warts.

"*One* commercial! For your uncle's company!" Hannah pushed Grace, who pushed her back. A wart-covered hand pulled a fistful of chin hair. Long, curling nails scratched at greenish skin. They pushed and pulled each other to the floor, where their wrestling brought them dangerously close to the edge of the platform.

Grace's hair, frizzy and gray, touched the water, and she screamed. Hannah held her down while the fish ate her hair.

Melody and Crow exchanged a look. They had to do something. She pulled Hannah back, and he helped Grace up. If anything, this made her scream more loudly.

"Get away from me!" Hannah yelled, struggling to free herself from Melody's hold.

"Let go of me!" Grace cried. She pushed Crow away. "This is all your fault!"

Hannah nodded, her large nose bobbing up and down. "Yeah. The two of you are probably working with the monster. Monsters always work together!"

Crow stepped backward, away from the girls who

had stopped attacking each other and now looked ready to attack him. With another step, he tripped over something. No—not something. Someone. Travis. Only a foot tall, he'd tied his shirt around him as a sort of robe, and the rest of his clothes sat in a heap.

Hannah lunged, and all Crow could see was nose. He rolled away just in time, and she landed on top of Travis, whose high-pitched scream could have made dogs cry.

Melody leaped onto a platform passing by. "Come on, Crow. Before it moves away."

Crow hesitated. He knew they were supposed to wait with the patience of a spider, but spiders didn't have to deal with Grace and Hannah. He jumped.

His left foot grazed the water, but the rest of him landed safely on the platform. He took off his shoe, worried that the fish still clung to it. The vicious little creatures had stayed in the water, though. Other than a large hole in the sole of his shoe, he was fine. He'd made it.

Grace and Hannah crouched, ready to jump. Panic filled Crow's mind. He'd made it onto one platform, but the next was farther away, and the one after that farther still. He'd never make it all the way to the exit. And the girls, sure that he was a monster, sure that he had something to do with their curse, might throw him into the water if they ever caught up. Even an un-dead boy couldn't survive being eaten.

"Don't leave me!" Travis cried, his voice high and tiny. "I can't jump that far."

With the platforms moving away, Grace and Hannah couldn't jump, either. They whispered to each other before sitting down next to the button. They pressed it for a long time, until the platform shrank to half its original size. Then, seeing that Melody had been right, they finally stopped. The two groups waited separately, occasionally sliding much closer than Crow would have liked.

CHAPTER TWENTY-FIVE

The wait seemed longer this time. Crow wondered whether, as punishment for jumping onto the next platform, they would be stuck there forever. Maybe it was better that way. Defeating the Meera seemed like an impossible feat.

But he had to try.

No longer fighting, Hannah and Grace sat leaning against each other. A lump of clothes that must have been Travis sat between them.

Crow couldn't help feeling sorry for them.

Before his death, he'd had a pretty good life. He was the captain of the academic bowl, the winner of the fourth-grade spelling bee, and the star of the school play. Friends always surrounded him, and in third grade, he'd gotten more Valentine's Day cards than anyone else in his class.

Luke hadn't gotten any cards that year. People had given him some; he just never received them. Someone had dumped all of his cards into Crow's bag. By the time Crow noticed that some of the cards were addressed to someone else, he'd already bragged about all the valentines he'd received. He couldn't admit the truth then, not even to stop Luke from crying in the corner.

He hadn't thought about that day for a long time. It had only been a prank. Crow didn't even know who'd done it—maybe someone trying for a laugh, maybe someone seeking revenge. It hadn't seemed important, not in light of everything that had happened.

Now he couldn't stop thinking about it.

Maybe Crow had never bullied anyone the way Luke and his friends did, but he hadn't always been nice, either. That didn't mean that he'd deserved to have his life ripped away from him, though. Nobody was perfect. The Meera should know that.

The slow back-and-forth movement of the floating platforms lulled everyone to sleep. Everyone except Crow, who never slept. Hours later, when the platforms lined up, he was the only one still awake.

He shook Melody's shoulder. She bolted upright, her eyes already wide open. She started to say something, but he silenced her with a finger to his mouth. He pointed to the platforms, and she nodded.

They tiptoed forward, silently agreeing not to wake the others. It was safer for everyone that way.

"Are you sure about this?" Melody whispered. They were standing in front of the door.

"Isn't it too late to change our minds?" Crow thought he could hear a low growling coming from the next room. The Meera was waiting for them.

"We'll be fine," he added, trying his best to sound more confident than he felt. "We just have to stick to the plan. Right?"

Melody nodded and handed him the backpack.

They entered the next room, where engravings of bees urged selflessness. The Meera stood in the center, its growl rising into a roar.

"Why have you come back? Didn't I give you everything you wished for?"

"You tricked us," Melody said, her voice quivering. "You cursed me."

"You cursed yourself, just as humans always do." Its eyes, blue with rectangular pupils, focused on Crow. "Almost always. Why have you come back? Surely those three vermin aren't worth your time."

"I thought you wanted us to be selfless," Crow said. "And no matter how awful they are, they don't deserve what you did to them. Nobody does. You have to stop."

"We can help you," Melody said. "You must hate that collar. We can help."

"*You* help *me*? Such arrogance." A laugh like a hyena's rolled out of the Meera's beak. "Humans always think they're better than everyone and everything else, but they aren't. My tests prove that."

"But why do you get to test people?" Crow asked. "Someone hurt you, so now you hurt everyone else? It isn't right. You have to stop."

"And I suppose you intend to make me?"

"Yes," Crow said, painfully aware of the Meera's single horn, sharp beak, and scorpion tail, all poised to strike. "You made a mistake. We know about the collar. Melody knows it's where your power comes from."

He removed a net from the backpack. Covered with oil, salt, and herbs, it was slick, and it almost slipped out of Crow's hands. He threw it over the Meera. Melody had promised the net would weaken the Meera enough to keep it from changing form—but not for long. They had to remove its collar before it had time to break free.

While the Meera struggled against the net, its beak already slicing the beginnings of a hole, Crow tossed Melody the last item from the bag. A hammer, treated with the same mixture of herbs, salt, and oil.

Hannah and Grace burst through the door. Travis,

the size of a thumb, rode on Hannah's shoulder. He was wearing some ribbon taken from Grace's Greek goddess dress, torn off and folded into a makeshift toga.

Grace grabbed Melody's arm. "You were going to leave without us!"

The hammer fell to the floor, Melody too distracted to catch it. She pushed Grace away, but it was too late. The Meera had broken free of the net.

Spider silk shot out from its torso, trapping Melody and Grace in the strong, sticky web. It did the same to Hannah and Travis before turning its attention to Crow. "You shouldn't have returned. Nobody receives a second wish."

"I don't want another wish," Crow said. He dodged a blast of webbing. "I don't want any wishes at all."

Only Melody truly understood the Meera's magic, but she had told Crow enough to defeat it. Hopefully. He just had to reach the hammer, which lay on the floor a few feet away. As more webbing shot toward him, he rolled out of the way and grabbed the hammer.

The Meera transformed into a small, feathered dinosaur. A velociraptor, Crow noted, only around thirty pounds but fast and deadly. He avoided the large claw on its hind legs, which the dinosaur used to kill its prey. When it charged at him, he used the hammer to swat it away.

The velociraptor cried in pain, then charged again. This time, a claw sliced through Crow's left arm before he managed to swat it away. He didn't know how long he could fight it off.

Even worse, now that the Meera had abandoned its hybrid form, he didn't know how to destroy its collar. He couldn't even see it anymore.

After another good swat at the velociraptor, he ran to Melody. She was still stuck in the web, futilely trying to tear her way out. Crow scratched at the web, too, without any more success. "What do I do?"

Her eyes widened. "Turn around!"

The Meera was transforming again. The feathers disappeared. The body grew, the tail becoming thick, the mouth enormous. Crow gulped. An allosaurus.

The allosaurus's giant jaws snapped at Crow, who avoided being eaten by jumping onto its snout. Its head thrashed back and forth, but he clung on. As he struggled to gain a better grip, he felt something hard and smooth around the beast's neck.

"It's still there," Melody said. "You can't see it, but you should be able to feel it."

The collar. The power source. It was right there; all Crow had to do was remove it.

But removing it wasn't that easy. The collar had grown with the rest of the beast. Crow held on to the allosaurus's nostril with one hand, using his other hand to pry the collar off with the claw of the hammer. The collar, strong and solid, resisted the attempt.

The allosaurus disappeared. Crow plummeted to the ground.

A fly buzzed away. The Meera was escaping.

Crow tried to stand—he needed to catch the Meera—but something was wrong with his leg. He looked down, expecting to find that another body part had fallen off. To his relief, his right leg was simply broken. Everything was still attached.

His decayed nerves registered nothing beyond a distant, dull ache. He pulled himself up, putting his weight on his left leg. The Meera was getting away. He had to stop it. Even without pain slowing him down, though, he couldn't move very fast. He hobbled forward. Not nearly fast enough.

Melody, still caught in the webbing, threw herself at the fly as it passed. Grace was dragged along, and the two fell in a tangled heap.

"I got it!" Melody yelled. "Hurry!"

Crow limped as fast as he could.

The fly was caught in the spiderweb. It buzzed angrily, unable to escape its own trap. Not in fly form, anyway.

Crow hesitated. If he attacked now, he'd kill the Meera. He'd never planned to do that.

"Smash it!" Grace yelled.

Melody jerked. "No! If you kill it, nothing will change!"

As she spoke, the Meera grew bigger. Its fragile insect wings became the strong, feathered wings of an owl. Its body stretched into the shape of a goat. A large scorpion tail, dripping with venom, rose from its backside. A sharp horn extended from its forehead.

The collar was visible once again.

The Meera tore itself free of the web. Its deadly tail arched forward, ready to sting Melody. She screamed.

Crow struck the collar with his hammer.

The Meera turned its attention to Crow, its stinger now aimed at him.

Melody had said that normally they'd never be able to break the dragon bone collar, but because of the anti-magic oil she'd concocted, they had a chance. He just had to hit it hard enough.

Before the Meera killed them.

Crow ducked out of the way of the stinger and struck the collar again. The Meera's claws slashed at his chest, tearing his shirt and slicing into his dead flesh. He raised the hammer again and brought it down on the collar with all his strength.

A crack formed in the dragon bone. With one more strike, the collar fell off.

The Meera went through a series of transformations—scorpion, dragon, fish, deer, mammoth, unicorn, crocodile, turtle, phoenix, goat, snake, and other creatures Crow couldn't identify—each one lasting a fraction of a second. When the changes stopped, it was an owl. Not a goat-scorpion-owl hybrid, but a regular, everyday owl. It flew away.

A wave of pain overwhelmed Crow. He passed out.

CHAPTER TWENTY-SIX

When Crow awoke, he noticed four things.

One, pain radiated from his leg. Not a dull ache, but real, burning, excruciating pain. The kind he hadn't felt in years.

Two, his skin was warm.

Three, something pounded against his chest in a vaguely familiar rhythm. Thump, thump. Thump, thump. Thump, thump.

Four, he'd been asleep. Unconscious, at least. That was nearly the same.

He opened his eyes and noticed several more things: the pinkish hue of his skin, the absence of maggots, the blood welling in a cut on his arm.

If it weren't for his broken leg, he would have jumped for joy. He tried to, despite the pain, but didn't get very far before collapsing back to the ground. The pain doubled, but it didn't matter.

In fact, it was wonderful.

He was alive.

The others had escaped from the webbing, although strands of spider's silk still clung to their hair and clothes. Travis was his normal size. Grace and Hannah glowed with beauty, despite Grace's uneven hair, still damaged from the fish attack.

Melody smiled. "It worked."

She held up the collar. It was pretty now that it wasn't attached to a monster. The silvery metal was so shiny that it reflected hints of pink, blue, purple, or green, depending on the way the light hit it. The engraved symbols formed a border around the lower and upper edges. "The Meera lost its magic. It's just an owl now."

"Its curses and wishes were undone?" Crow asked. "All of them?"

Melody's grin grew larger. "Just like I told you would happen. How does it feel?"

"Good." He winced. "Painful. How do we get out of here?"

"Not through the wall," Melody said. "Now that the Meera's magic is gone, so is the shortcut. I know because I spent ten minutes trying to walk through solid wall." She rubbed her forehead. "Very solid. We'll have to go back the way we came."

Crow's heart beat a little faster. The way they came had rickety bridges, chasms that could only be crossed by leaping, and walls that had to be scaled. He couldn't do any of that with a broken leg.

"But just into the next room," she added quickly. "There's another shortcut. A nonmagical one. I saw it on the way in, when an illusion was masking it—and locking it. The Meera had them all over the place. That was how it got around so easily without being seen."

Crow breathed a sigh of relief, and another wave of excitement coursed through him. He was breathing! He was alive!

While Melody led the way, Grace and Hannah helped him walk, acting as his crutches.

"Thanks," he said.

Grace looked like she wanted to speak, but her lips were pressed tightly together. Hannah mumbled something incomprehensible.

"What?" Crow asked. He started to check his ears for maggots but stopped himself. That wasn't a problem he'd have to deal with anymore.

"They want to say they're sorry," Melody said. "Right?"

"Yeah," said Grace. "I'm sorry I kicked you."

Travis and Hannah nodded. All three of them were looking at the floor. Crow wondered what Melody had said to them while he was unconscious. He gave her a questioning glance, but she just smiled.

In the next room, the rectangular platforms still formed a straight line from one door to the other. There was a third door, too. Crow could see it now, but he still couldn't reach it—not without wading through the pool of killer fish.

Something splashed.

Melody had fallen into the water.

"I'll help you!" Crow yelled, though he wasn't sure how much help he'd be with a broken leg.

Melody laughed and splashed water at him. "It's just regular water with regular fish now. The magic that made them deadly is gone. We tested it while you were unconscious. We were getting ready to carry you out of here when you finally woke up."

Crow watched her for a moment. She certainly didn't look like she was being eaten alive. He eased himself in slowly with Grace and Hannah's help, careful not to put any weight on his broken leg. Travis followed after a lengthy pause.

The door led to a dark staircase, which led to a sewer grate, which led to the park. The sun had set, long ago by the looks of it. The rain had stopped, but clouds still covered the sky, blocking out the moon and stars. The resulting darkness meant that Crow couldn't see anything unless someone shined a flashlight directly on it.

Including the source of that nearby rustling. He gulped. Was the Meera back for revenge already? Sure, it was just a regular owl now, but even a nonmagical owl had sharp claws and a beak.

But owls didn't produce heavy footsteps, which was what Crow heard next. He took a deep breath. "Who's there?"

"Crow? Is that you? It's me, Luke."

Melody shined her flashlight in the direction of the voice. It was Luke, all right.

"I came to the park like we agreed, but I didn't see you anywhere. I've been waiting for hours." His clothes were damp from the rain. He wrapped his arms around himself and shivered. "But I guess you guys went without me. Why did you do that?"

"You just had to go down the grate and catch up with us," Melody said. "Couldn't someone as smart as you supposedly are figure that out? Anyway, you were late. You got scared and left them the first time. How were we supposed to know you hadn't done it again?"

Hannah half laughed, half snorted.

"You little coward," Grace said.

"I didn't know I was friends with a chicken," Travis said. "Maybe I won't be anymore."

"Oh, like the three of you were any better," Melody said. "When the Meera took Luke, you couldn't run away fast enough. You *really* couldn't, since it caught you."

That silenced everyone for a while.

"But you're okay, right?" Luke asked, his voice softer than usual. Less certain.

Melody and Crow took turns filling him in on what had happened. When they got to the end, Melody held up the Meera's cracked collar, which glowed faintly against the surrounding darkness. She wouldn't let Luke touch it despite his repeated attempts.

"How does that thing work?" Luke asked.

Melody traced her fingers along the inscriptions. "The symbols are from the fairy language, and the metal is actually dragon bone. Before, I could read what the symbols meant, but now . . . It's all fading so quickly. As far as I could tell, a wizard made it and put it on a regular owl, turning it into a magical beast it could control."

"So where's the wizard now?"

"I don't know," Melody said. "Maybe he died. The Meera didn't seem to be taking orders from anyone."

"Does the collar still work?" Luke asked. "If you put it around an animal, will it become a monster you can control?"

"I don't know." She stared at the collar, then shook her head. "I understood this all so well, but already everything's fuzzy. I don't know what would happen if I put this on an animal." She smiled. "Think I should try it on you?"

No longer interested in touching the collar, Luke

stepped back. He squinted at Crow. "I don't get it. Why are you alive again? Your parents' wish brought you back to life, right? So shouldn't you be dead now? Like, really dead?"

"You honestly don't know, do you?" Crow's leg hurt. His entire body ached with exhaustion. He wanted to go home, not stand around and talk. But he also wanted Luke to know the truth. "Back in elementary school, you complained to your parents about me." He waited, searching Luke's face for a flash of memory.

It never came, so Crow continued. "We were both competing in the school spelling bee. Back then, you were different. You studied hard, and you were a runner-up. I got first place. The same thing happened in the academic bowl. We were both class captains, but my class won. And there was the school play. I got the lead. You were my understudy."

Finally, realization dawned on Luke's face.

But his memory of the events was probably skewed and incomplete. Crow told him the rest of the story, exactly as his father had told him.

"I remember when my parents disappeared at the park," Luke said. "I had to spend the night at Travis's. They came back the next day, but they never told me where they'd been. They never said anything about the Meera."

Crow wasn't surprised. His parents hadn't told him

much, either, not until they had to. "They probably wanted to protect you."

He shook his head. "You're lying. Why should I believe you?"

"I don't know," Crow said. He had more to say, but he paused. Something was flying over the park— something shaped very much like an owl.

Or a pigeon. Or nothing at all. The pain and fatigue might have been causing Crow to see things. He took a deep breath and finished the story. "But it's the truth. That's why I'm alive now. The Meera's magic brought me back to life, but it was also what killed me—because of you."

The light reflected off something falling down Luke's cheek. A tear. "It wasn't my fault," he whispered.

"No, it wasn't," Crow said. "You didn't know what would happen. Your parents didn't, either."

An owl hooted. Definitely an owl this time. Crow looked around, but he couldn't find it. That meant it could be anywhere. "We should go. A lot of people are looking for the three of you."

Every light in the Darlingsons' house was on.

Melody helped Crow to the porch; the others had gone to their own homes already. If they followed Melody's advice, they'd tell the authorities that they had gone down into the underground tunnels and gotten lost. It might not have been the most believable story, but it was certainly easier to accept than the truth.

The front door flew open before they even reached it. Mrs. Darlingson stood there. Her mouth opened, but the words she had planned never made it past her throat. When she saw her son, she fell to her knees. Tears streamed down her face. While she gave Crow a long, wet hug, Melody slipped away.

CHAPTER TWENTY-SEVEN

Crow observed the neighborhood from his bedroom window. The sun shined brightly in a clear blue sky. Cars peeled out of driveways as their owners rushed to work. Luke and Travis were already waiting at the bus stop. Grace and Hannah, currently walking down the sidewalk, would soon join them, and Melody was just opening her front door.

Mrs. Darlingson grabbed Crow's hand and pulled him away, gently because of his cast. "You'd better hurry. You don't want to miss the bus on your first day of school." She frowned. "Although I still think you should wait a while longer. Until your leg heals, at least. And it might be easier to wait until next September, so you won't have to start midyear. You'll have a lot of catching up to do, and I already have your homeschool lessons planned. I can call the school right now to make the necessary arrangements."

"No," Crow said quickly. He adjusted his crutches under his arms and hobbled to the door. "I'm ready."

Downstairs, the front door opened. "Is Crow still here? I've been running late all morning—coffeemaker got clogged, car keys went missing, hit every red light in Blaze. I hope I haven't missed him."

"Dad?" Crow turned to Mrs. Darlingson. "You didn't say Dad was coming."

Mr. Darlingson bounded up the stairs. "Of course I came. I couldn't miss your first day at middle school, could I?"

A huge grin spread over Crow's face. He hadn't seen his father since the hospital.

His cast and crutches made going downstairs difficult, but he refused his parents' many offers of help. He'd have to deal with stairs at school, so he might as well start practicing.

Mrs. Darlingson handed him his backpack. "I've made a lunch for you. Peanut butter and strawberry jam. You like that, right? You used to like it, I remember."

Crow slung the backpack over his shoulders and readjusted his crutches.

"Tonight, we can go out to dinner to celebrate your first day," Mrs. Darlingson added. "How does that sound?"

"All three of us?" Crow asked.

She hesitated for only a moment. "Yes, all three of us. Melody, too, if you want. You pick the restaurant."

Crow smiled. "That sounds good."

The bus was already at the bus stop, but the driver waited patiently as Crow hobbled down the sidewalk.

"Hey, Crow!" Melody yelled, running forward to meet him. She helped him get on the bus, and this time, Crow didn't mind needing assistance. She'd be there at school to help him, too. That was what best friends were for.

Luke, Travis, Hannah, and Grace had already taken their seats in the back. They waved awkwardly, and Luke gestured to an empty seat.

"Let's just sit here," Crow said, still near the front of the bus. He didn't want to walk farther than he had to, especially in the narrow bus aisle.

He'd see Luke later, anyway. Luke had been coming over almost every day, just to hang out. He'd even signed Crow's cast. Crow suspected that although Luke was popular and had never had to deal with maggots or foul odors, he got lonely sometimes. Maybe having friends wasn't as important as having the right friends.

Crow and Melody sat down and compared schedules. They had the same lunch period and a few of the same classes.

"I can point out the werewolf teacher," Melody said. "Although he looks normal to me now, thank goodness. I wrote some stuff down when I was under the curse, so if I keep rereading it, I won't completely forget." She bit her lower lip. "Um, have you noticed anything strange since that night?"

Crow frowned. "Like what?"

"An owl."

"It was in the park," Crow said. "I heard it while we were talking to Luke. But I haven't heard or seen it since. Have you?"

She nodded. "Every night. It sits on a branch outside my window. I think it knows I have the collar, even though I put it away somewhere safe, with lots of the oil mixture. My entire room smells like basil now."

"But it's just an owl now, right? It can't do anything."

Melody smiled. "Right."

Crow hesitated. "Have you heard from the brownie yet?" If she had, he couldn't imagine that it had been good news. If the brownie had found her mother, she would have said something.

"No. And now that I can't see magic, I don't think I'm going to." She looked down at her lap. "I don't think it would have helped anyway. Some things can't be solved with magic."

The bus pulled up in front of the school, a massive two-story building that Crow knew he'd get lost in. He and Melody got off last, after everyone who wasn't slowed down by a broken leg.

Everything made noise—the bus engine, the warning bell, his classmates. The racket overwhelmed Crow, who was used to his quiet home. It was so loud that he couldn't be sure, but he thought he heard something else.

A nearby hooting.

He paused in front of the massive school doors. He didn't see anything, but there were plenty of hiding spots nearby.

"Is something wrong?" Melody asked.

"No," Crow said. He smiled. So what if an owl was watching? "Let's go. I don't want to be late for class."

ACKNOWLEDGMENTS

I want to thank my husband, who always believed in me, even when I didn't, and who let me bounce ideas off him. My wonderful agent, David Dunton, has also earned my never-ending gratitude. Thanks to everyone at Crown, especially Phoebe Yeh and Rachel Weinick, who offered amazing insight that helped me make this book the best it could be. Thank you to Yoko Tanaka, an extremely talented artist, for transforming my words into pictures. Finally, I need to thank everyone who reads this book. I hope you enjoy it.